The Edge of Carmel

The Fourth Jaden Steele
Carmel Mystery

Barbara Chamberlain

Cups of Gold Publishing Company

Los Gatos, California

The Jaden Steele Carmel Mysteries

A Slice of Carmel
Slash and turn
The Sword of Smuggler's Point
The Edge of Carmel

The Flight of Alpha One
Award winning juvenile fantasy
Ages 9+ Recommended by
The National League of American Pen
Women

ISBN 978-0-9835395-2-0
First North American Edition Copyright 2020

1. Mystery and Detective Stories.
2. Carmel-Fiction
3. Jaden Steele (Fictitious Character)

Many thanks to my family

and friends who kept asking

Where is your next book?

A special thanks to

Santa Clara Pen Women President

Luanna Leisure for

Technical Problem Solving

Prologue

The living sea is like a moody person. Some days the ocean yells loudly at the world by its continual pounding on the shore. The waves swell high, shouting "touch me at our peril." The tide laps up to the highest water mark. The waves can trap some unsuspecting soul in a vicious current from which there is no escape. Other days smooth, gentle waves caress the shore under a bright sun. A pair of dolphins glides near the shore, diving through the schools of fish for their lunch. Their sea bird companions hover over them, gulping up leftovers. Surfers ride the waves. Laughing children play tag with the white bubbling foam. With their plastic shovels and buckets they make castles in the wet sand. The castles will be washed away by the next tide. But with a new day a new pod of children will make fresh castles in the sand at the edge of the living, ever restless sea

THE EDGE OF CARMEL

Barbara Chamberlain

Jaden peered down the stairway. She could only see splotches of drying blood that must have sprayed helter-skelter as the body fell. She started down carefully, avoiding the blood that certainly would be evidence. Everything whirled around her as though she were on an out of control carousel. Her hand slipped into her pocket to feel the Monarch knife that was her old friend. The world finally stopped whirling. Breathing deeply, she steadied herself against the rail. Jaden did not need protection from a dead body.

She spotted a hand, the five fingers spread out on the dark laminate flooring. The hand seemed to grow larger and larger until her reaction was to whip out and click open her torsion blade knife.

The steel glinted in the light. The flash made her blink. When she opened her eyes the unmoving hand had returned to normal size. The pale fingers were sticking out of a plaid blanket that had been thrown over the still body. Jaden imagined that the crime scene had already been disturbed enough. Where was the knife?

She took the deepest breath possible to steady herself as she reached the last step. The pungent odor of blood made her struggle not to vomit. The blanket hid the body for a few seconds before Jaden forced herself to lift the soft corner to reveal the entire corpse. Someone had tried to contain the blood flow by placing rolled up towels around the top of the body. They were white towels dyed true blood red.

Here was dead as dead could be.

The Edge of Carmel

Four months earlier

The small brass bell attached to the doorknob rang as a familiar gray-haired woman entered the shop carrying a sunny yellow orchid. The petals of the three flowering spikes were striped with red. As if to accentuate the beauty, the edges of the petals were spotted with the same red.

"This will add color to your display, Jaden." Ruth Spaulding put the plant in the window display of the cutlery shop, A Slice of Carmel. "Brightness for the knife display. This paring knife is lovely." She fingered the edge. I love sharp edges. "They cut so quickly."

Jaden understood. Her own grandfather was a butcher who also made knives. He taught her to love and to respect them. *The most valuable tool ever.*

"Did you bring any of your cutlery for me to sharpen today?"

An useless question. Ruth always had knives to sharpen. She owned the most honed blades in Carmel-By-The-Sea. Most knife owners knew dull blades could be dangerous.. To her it was like a religious duty.

"Oh, yes." Ruth reached into her large patchwork bag and pulled out a flat newspaper wrapped package. Almost like a magician she unwrapped it in one turn to reveal two large knives. They were from A Slice of Carmel, an excellent brand of German steel.

Jaden knew that they would still be sharp enough for most of the restaurant cooks in the village by the sea. Not Ruth. She must have invented the words, super sharp.

"No use having them if they are not razor sharp." Ruth's clear, sky blue eyes sparkled. "And for preparing anything for canning, too. So easy with a sharp edge. Dull edges are worthless."

"Do you have any more of your prize winning pickles?" Jaden took the knives.

"Not yet. I've ordered two lugs of cucumbers but have to drive to Gilroy to pick them up. A friend and I will do that Wednesday. The best pickles are from fresh picked cukes. Hard to find farmers who will get up at five in the morning to pick fresh for you. The best pickles need to be brined the same day they are picked."

"You should know. First prize at the fair for how many years is it now?"

"Ten," she said with a sweet smile.

Ruth's pickles were so popular that she could easily charge $20 for a quart. They were not like other pickles. They were crisper with a deep dill flavor. Once you tasted one you were hooked. "No other pickles compare with yours. They're addicting. Will you ever tell your secret brine recipe?"

"It always will be a mystery." Her sweet smile lit the shop. "It's my spice."

Nothing would ever pry the recipe from her either. At her age, which Jaden guessed to be about seventy-five, the ingredients would probably die with her.

The Edge of Carmel

Too bad she had to keep up these orchid deliveries at her age. Many local seniors augmented their social security income one way or another. Several of her customers like Ruth were living on the edge of Carmel, on the edge of a town of mostly very well-off citizens. The "edgers" just got by one way or the other. Many were like Ruth, from families who had bought homes fifty years earlier and found themselves in million dollar homes with small incomes. Being from an older generation they often did not want to ask for help. Ruth lived literally and financially at the edge of Carmel.

Rumors were that Ruth's husband had run off with someone about fifteen years earlier. No children. She lived on the edge of Carmel in a house that was built into a hill next to Monterey. The backyard was a steep drop off. Metal pillars supported the back of the house. It must have two or even three levels of stairs. Jaden picked up an orchid there one day when Ruth was not feeling well. Every window of the living room was full of blooming orchids in a rainbow of colors. She could not believe how beautiful and varied they were.

Jaden remembered how she took a deep breath of admiration when she saw them. When the flowers of the orchid in the cutlery shop window fell off, there was no way it would ever bloom again for Jaden. Ruth would bring the plant back to her house and it would magically send out a new spike or two and bloom again for her.

White, pink, orchid lavender, pale yellow, yellow with red stripes, sunny yellow like the one she had brought in today.

Jaden drew the blade down the file and tested it on a strip of paper. The blade slid down easily. *It would cut through meat like butter. Even many bones. The tip was so sharp that she did not dare touch it.* She shivered briefly. Her grandfather showed her how to sharpen. Probably fifty knives of all sizes hung everywhere in his shop. People came from all over to buy them.

After she bought the business, it came as a surprise to find out that his knives were collector's items. She only owned two. Against her grandmother's protests, her grandfather taught her how to throw. She carried her monarch torsion blade usually in her pocket. It was not really all for protection. Her husband, Brett, had the knife specially made for her. This was all she had left of him besides their wedding picture. The Monarch was like an old friend, a good luck charm. "You have such a talent with the phalaenopsis. This plant is beautiful, Ruth."

"Thanks, dear. Could I sit down for a minute? It's been a busy day and I'm not getting any younger. Many days I have to take afternoon naps."

Her chest was visibly heaving in and out.

"Would you like some water?"

"No, thanks, Jaden. I'll just catch my breath. I have one more delivery to make."

Her face was paler than normal. *She needs to retire completely.*

At least Jaden knew what happened to her own husband. Poor Ruth would probably never know. The rumors persisted for fifteen years. People said that Ruth would not talk about it. Rumors were that the man just took off one day with a lot of their joint bank account.

"They are like razors now. Be careful." Jaden wrapped the two knives back in the newspaper and put them back in Ruth's colorful patchwork bag..

The bell attached to the door of the shop rang again. A short, thin woman dressed in gray slacks and a matching gray shirt came into the shop. Laura Morgan did not take off her sunglasses. She smiled nervously. Even with the sunglasses Jaden saw that the left side of her face in front of her ear was bruised. "Laura, what happened?"

"Oh," Laura looked at the floor. "It was so clumsy of me. I left the kitchen cupboard door open and walked right into it. Looks worse than it is, really. Broke my glasses, too." She removed her sunglasses. "These have my prescription until I can order a new pair of my regular glasses. I need to wait until the finances improve."

Jaden and Ruth exchanged a quick glance. "Laura, I have several pairs of reading glasses." Jaden opened the desk drawer and took out a pair. "If you can read with these 2.50s, you can borrow or keep them."

"Really, Jaden? Thank you so much. Just what I need. You won't miss them?"

It wasn't long ago that Laura came in with a broken arm. That time she said she fell off her front step. Accidents do happen, but didn't that cast just come off? Laura and her husband, Jeff Morgan, ran a souvenir shop, The Village Gift Store, near Seventh and Dolores. Jaden thought that Laura really ran the shop because Jeff spent a lot of time in the Carmel

Pub halfway between here and their shop. Jaden always felt uneasy around him. Even worse, he usually smelled like alcohol. She knew she should not pay attention to her sixth sense, the one that made the back of her neck feel cold. Sometimes, though, the gray to black cloudiness overwhelmed everything else. That meant the nagging nightmare memories were bubbling to the surface. Jaden grabbed the nearest display case to steady herself.

When she was trapped in the caves below the Bartlett house in Big Sur she knew the evil spirits were trying to kill her.. There were malevolent spirits who caused the death of two innocent people in Big Sur two centuries earlier. Jaden learned that evil is always present, lurking, delighting in causing problems and death if it can. That feeds its ego and delights in misery. There is more than enough unnecessary cruelty in the world already without the spirits from the past merging with today's evil.

All of her memories told her that the good spirits in the house, the ones who wanted her to solve the cold case mystery, helped her escape.

During what she thought were her last moments Jaden also learned something that she had tried to repress. The truth seemed disloyal to her first husband, a man who had been her best friend.

There was a new love in her life. He made her happier than she had been in years. After she moved from Nebraska, Jaden discovered that the reason she moved, her romantic lover, turned out to be a lying womanizer. Jaden could have easily killed him herself, but someone beat her to it.

Never admitted that to anyone but herself. Jaden wondered if she had an evil streak lurking deep inside of her. Some circumstances could drive a person to an act of insanity.

In Carmel she had made so many good friends--Bobbi Jones, Hal Lamont, who owned their small shopping corner, Ruth Stennis and her son, retired General Stennis, MacKenzie Anderson, her lawyer, who owned a vacation condo here, Sydney and Kyle, who operated the Mad Hatter's Café.

Looking at Laura she sensed that the woman badly needed a friend.

"Laura, would you like some coffee or tea? I have some of that raspberry tea from the Mad Hatter's Cafe."

"No, thank you," Laura's red rimmed eyes darted back and forth. "I just came in to pick up the knives I left for sharpening. The shop is closed right now and I want to open it up before the noon crowd comes in."

"How is business?" Ruth asked.

Laura sighed.

"That bad?" Ruth put her large handbag over her shoulder.

"It's bad. Not enough to pay expenses. By next month we won't be able to pay the lease. We'll have to go out of business. Jeff's been upset because his dream was running for city council. There's no way we can afford to stay here. I don't know where we can go." Her final words waivered, like she was describing someone who died. She obviously was fighting back tears.

Jaden understood perfectly, except for the politics part. That would be a big headache. She had been lucky to stay in business herself. That was because she had a reasonable lease agreement for three years from the former owner, Hal Lamont. So many businesses in Carmel came and went. Income has to exceed outgo. The term "high rent" probably originated here. Hal was an exception. "I'm still making money," he told them. He owned four businesses, six apartments, and practically a city block in Carmel that he purchased decades earlier. The wise investments obviously brought him a handsome income.

"Sit down, Laura." Jaden took Laura's shoulder gently and led her to a chair by the window. "A cup of ice water is just what you need. The store can wait for a few minutes."

The water seemed to revive her. When she left, Ruth walked out with her.

Jaden felt angry because she knew Laura was not telling the truth about her injuries. She was not a clumsy woman. Jaden's friend, Bill, a Carmel police officer, would be sympathetic but could not do much without a complaint from Laura. If the woman had not complained by now, she probably never would.

Why will some women not fight back against a life of terror? Bobbi told her it was because they are brainwashed. "One day it was like all the gray clouds parted. I saw everything he did for what it was. But after I applied for divorce, the terror and the bullying and stalking did not stop."

Later, when Jaden talked to Bill about the situation, he confirmed what she already knew. Nothing he could do.

"I can't help worrying. And I feel frustrated and helpless."

"Dear, I understand." His fingers gently brushed back her bangs, which eternally wanted to fall over her eyes. "We can't do anything unless she complains. And even then, these guys keep on with their behavior. Your worry is understandable."

"She won't complain." Jaden stared into the mist rising from her coffee. "I don't understand it, but Bobbi does. She felt the same way for a long time. If she would do better, then he would not hurt her. If she worked harder, tried to please him more, he would not beat her. When she finally wanted to get away she was trapped. Her husband would not let her go. He always blamed the beatings on her. For a long time, she believed that. 'You get beaten down in more ways than one. It's hard to explain.' "

"Sounds typical," Bill told Jaden. "Wife beaters are cowards. They don't let go."

"I think I'll explain the situation to Bobbi. Maybe she can make an impression. Try to get Laura help. What I do know is that Bobbi does not want to talk about what happened to her. She calls it her nightmare days that were so difficult to forget. If I explain, though, I'm sure she will help."

Bill kissed her gently. She snuggled up against him and relaxed. "Will you stay?"

He whispered, "Until you go to sleep. I have paperwork to do. Can stay in my apartment and work on the desktop. Call me and I will be right here."

She felt like Ruth—needing more sleep than she did even a year ago. Her mind would not stop reliving the conversation with Laura. Jaden used several of her go to sleep practices until one finally worked. She conjured up Bill's unusually smiling face. That relaxed so much that she fell asleep.

When Jaden woke up about 3:30 a.m., she was asleep on the sofa with her grandmother's wedding ring patterned quilt tucked around her. The heirloom was a great comforter that always relaxed her. She could remember her grandmother tucking her in with this quilt.

Jaden slept a little the rest of the morning worrying about Laura. She called Bobbi at 8 a.m. to explain the situation.

For a long few seconds her friend did not say a word. Finally she nodded her head.

"I'll try for you, Jaden. I know exactly how it is. But if she is not willing to help herself, nothing I say will convince her. These men have a way of brainwashing their victims. Now it's clear.. When I was in that same type of situation, I was helpless. Or I thought I was helpless."

"Thanks, Bobbi. Just do your best. That's all you can do. Thanks so much. "

Bobbi did not want to bring up the memories of her nightmare past. She kept telling herself this visit was for Jaden. When she thought Jaden had disappeared at the Bartlett house in Big Sur, she prayed. "I'll do anything. Please save my best friend in the world." Seeing Laura was her way of helping Jaden. Until she moved to Carmel, she had had no friends. Her husband had seen to that.

She called Laura.

Late in the afternoon Bobbi was having coffee with Laura in the upstairs apartment above the gift shop. She was here because of her friendship with Jaden. Bobbi hated reliving her nightmare past. Her concern about the woman with her mushroomed. The bruise on the side of her face looked all too familiar. Bobbi winced as though she had been hit herself. She almost felt the blow.

"Laura, have you heard anything about me? About my past?"

The other woman shook her head. She closed her eyes. When she opened them, they were filling with tears. She was hurting. This brought back the memory of pain that Bobbi felt five years ago. It could have been yesterday. She could relive every horrible moment like she was watching a movie. Now Bobbi could see that she should have left her husband the first time he hit her. He always said that he was sorry, but if she had not let the dinner get cold or cooked hamburgers when he wanted steak.

She made him angry...Everything was her fault. The memory of how she believed those deliberate lies made her shudder.

Bobbi heard her own voice tremble. "Let me tell you my story. I understand what you are going through. It takes a lot of courage to cope."

Laura took a sip of coffee. "I know what you are thinking. He doesn't mean it, really. He gets so frustrated...drinks. The business...all the bills we can't pay...I'm working hard to keep it going."

She's carrying the whole load.

Bobbi reached out for Laura's hands. "I used to feel the same way. Tried so hard. After working all day I fixed what I thought was a good meal. For some reason every meal had something wrong with it. One time he threw the plate on the floor. The beans were raw. The next night the squash was too mushy. That time he hit me on my right shoulder. Couldn't use my arm for a week. I didn't do or say anything to anyone."

A tear rolled down Laura's face. Bobbi knew what she was feeling. The desire to take her out of this shop, this place, overwhelmed her. After Bobbi realized she needed to escape this man and disappear, how different her life might have been. Her efforts to flee were always thwarted. When she finally woke up, she applied for a court order and a divorce. Her husband paid no attention to the order. His own created disaster ended his life.

His phone messages were consistent, "Don't think you are going to get a dime from me! Don't think you are safe, either."

And she knew she wasn't.

She could not sleep. Every noise at night made her jump or tremble. She lost ten pounds because of a constant stomachache. Bobbi felt as though she were the only person in the world. Isolated. The police could not help unless she could prove he actually did try to harm her. By then she knew it would be too late.

Bobbi looked down to see that her own hands were trembling.

Fine help she was to Laura.

She thought the nightmare time was buried deep in her memory. Maybe it would never go away. *At least I can try to help Laura. How can I get through to her?*

"Bobbi, I had no idea," Laura looked at her with sympathetic brown eyes. "You are so beautiful and together. You have everything going for you."

"It was not always that way, believe me. When my husband came home, I was terrified that he might not like dinner."

Laura sighed. "What can I do? Jeff does not like me to invite friends over. He won't like it if he finds you here."

Bobbi sighed because that sounded so familiar. Her husband never welcomed any of her friends. He had something bad to say about each one of them. Mention anyone's name and there was something wrong with them. Finally, she realized he was lying.

"Here is my card. If anything happens call 911 right away. Or call me or Jaden if you need to talk to someone or need help."

Bobbi thought, *She needs help now.* Laura hesitated and then took the card. She opened a cupboard door in the workroom and put the card in her purse.

"He's unhappy because he was trying to impress the local politicians to run for office. At the same time mention any of their names and he says something bad about all of them.

"There are places you can go. When I was abused, I didn't know that. There's a place in Monterey. A safe house. I'll find out the phone number for you. It's confidential."

Bobbi clenched her teeth. This was not going well. Laura was too beaten down. She knew Jaden would want to hear everything that happened. Her friend was sensitive enough to realize Laura needed help. Bobbi's mind raced on how to put a positive spin on this so far depressing conversation.

"Laura, you could come home with me and you could rest."

"Oh, there is too much to do here. The shop. I couldn't leave right now."

Bobbi took a deep breath. "All right." She really wanted to scream at the woman.

The poor woman winced when Bobbi hugged her at the top of the stairs.

After she left Laura's apartment Bobbi relived the whole conversation on her walk back to the library. For some reason she looked back over her shoulder several times. *Imagined someone was following her. That was silly on these crowded sidewalks.* She did not have the confidence that Laura realized her situation was dangerous. This was so like what had happened to her that it was giving her a dull headache. Bobbi felt unsettled and almost wished she had not gone. But the effort had been made. She had given Laura her best advice. The whole time her instincts told her to make Laura leave the gift shop with her and never go back. The whole conversation made her stomach knot. For Bobbi it was those memories that she wanted to bury. Jaden was so different. While she had lived through several problems, including the death of her husband, Bobbi knew Jaden would never stay with an abusive man. She would leave the first time he hit her.. Her skill with knives would be enough to put off anyone.

When the trial was over and Bobbi was acquitted of murder, she was mad at herself for ever tolerating the abusive situation. She sniffled and stopped next to a gallery stoe window to dig a Kleenex out of her purse. Going back to the library in tears was not what she wanted.

Her cell phone rang. It was David. Since she and Jaden visited Big Sur the year before, she and David Bartlett had become good friends. David was a rock when they all thought Jaden was lost. Now he wanted more from Bobbi than being good friends.

"Hello, David."

"Hi, beautiful. How are you?"

"Ok. I'm walking back to work."

"Where have you been?"

"I'll tell you about it next time I see you. It's a long story."

"You sound upset."

"You're right about that."

"I have to come up to Monterey this Saturday and want to take you out to dinner. Maybe on the wharf? The ocean is always calming."

"I'd love that, David."

"I'll pick you up about five o'clock. Why don't you ask Jaden and Bill if they can come with us?"

"OK. Sounds great."

"Goodbye, Bobbi."

"See you Saturday."

She stared at the phone for a few seconds. David had a talent for lifting her spirits. He asked her to marry him and live at the remote estate on Smuggler's Point. She had fought off the temptation so far. The big problem was that David wanted to stay in Big Sur. Bobbi had friends and a job here in Carmel. She thought about David a lot, though. To be honest, she admitted that she loved him.

And the isolated Bartlett estate was as close to getting away from the world as possible. Her terrifying marriage and her murder trial with its ugly publicity hurt her badly. Talking to Laura made the waterfall of painful memories wash over her until she had to wipe away the tears.

She swallowed hard and opened the back door to the busy library, to her reference librarian's job. There was nothing better for her than staying as busy as possible.

Jaden woke to the sensation that someone was in the room with her. She dug into her pocket for her knife. A strong hand restrained her and the other hand brushed back her hair.

Bill kissed her softly at first and then deepened the kiss until she forgot completely about her Monarch knife or anything else. She put her free arm around his neck.

He pulled back and said, "May I let go of your hand now?"

She smiled. "I guess you are safe."

"Remember I know how fast you can pull that knife out. Why are you napping on your lunch hour? If you stayed up late last night, I should have been with you."

"I would not have gotten any sleep."

The cell phone rang. Jaden picked it up.

"Yes, Bobbi." Jaden listened to the whole story of her visit to Laura. The more she listened, the more she frowned. Laura should have listened to the librarian.

"Bobbi, you did your best. Laura has to take responsibility for herself. She knows that we are here to help if she wants. Thanks for seeing her. You did the best you could. You are an angel."

She pressed the red button.

Bill guessed, "It sounds like Bobbi was not too happy with the visit."

"Laura has been intimidated for years. You know the routine too well, I'm guessing. Somehow she's made to feel responsible for everything that Jeff does."

"It's the usual routine. These guys are so worthless. Even after they finally are arrested, the women take them back. I've never known any of the men to change their behavior. That's my experience anyway. The women or what's even worse, the women and the children have to get away."

Jaden felt herself trembling. She groped for the chair and sat down. This had happened usually with no explanation after her ordeal of being trapped in the network of caves underneath the Bartlett house on Smuggler's Point. Going into the caves alone was her own fault. She took months to recover to probably sixty per cent of her former self. Sometimes for a few seconds the darkness of the cave would surround her, trap her in a black world with no escape. Sometimes she imagined she saw clouds of mean, aggressive black crows threatening to engulf her.

Then brilliant flashes of light would make her close her eyes until it all went away. When she opened her eyes, her normal world would return. Jaden worried about these episodes. She did not want to tell the doctor. She did not need any more pills than she was taking.

Vitamins were all she wanted to use.

Bill's comforting arm slipped around her. He kissed her. "Jaden, you need to rest more. I can tell Hal to close the shop early for you if he doesn't want to stay until five."

"Hal did so much while I was in bed. He thought he had sold the shop and retired."

"He is the type who never retires. Look at all the charity work he is doing. And he owns this whole block in Carmel. He's busy just collecting rents."

Jaden, normally stubborn, said, "I will lie down for an hour. If you could tell Hal that I will call him if I can't go down to the shop. He and Sandy might be doing something tonight."

Bill stared at her with those penetrating dark, almost black, eyes. By this time he knew he could not argue with her. When she was missing and then found close to death, the thought of losing her almost made him lose his mind. Bill forgot about everything else in his life. He prayed for her to recover. When she did, he wasted no more time telling her how he felt. Since then his life had been happier than he had ever been. The worry about Jaden's health was constant. The doctor said she would take a long time to recover. He was right.

I want to take her away somewhere, maybe Hawaii, some remote spot, for a complete rest. And a honeymoon, if she would say yes.

He realized that besides his concern for her he wanted to get her away from everyone else for his own selfish reasons. His courage failed him every time he wanted to ask her to marry him. The fear of rejection stopped him.

"You look pretty serious," Jaden commented. "Can you tell me?"

"I want you to get better," he answered. "And I want us to get away."

"I am recovering, but wish I had more energy. There isn't any magic pill."

"Are you taking those vitamins?"

"Of course. With you hovering over me I'm eating very well. Putting on weight."

"You've got to stop worrying about other people like Laura. I know how you are. You get one thing in your mind and you never quit. That's why you got yourself trapped in those smuggling caves." He had not meant to say that for about the fiftieth time. It always slipped out.

Bill realized that he could not change her personality. Jaden said she was trying to change after almost dying in the caves under David Bartlett's house. At age thirty-four her personality, sometimes curious to the point of obsession, was probably not going to change.

The only plus about the event was that Jaden did solve the cold case mystery of Rosalba Bartlett's death. And her friend, Bobbi, and David Bartlett, were drawn to each other. Bobbi was happier than he had ever seen her. Jaden commented on it.

"I would miss Bobbi," she told him.

"She would be only thirty miles from here. Not quite the end of the world."

"The road down there is not easy. Winding and slow. Sometimes it seems like the end of the world. I think she and David really are in love, though. Most of my reservations are selfish. And you're right. Not like she's going to England or China."

"After everything she's been through, Bobbi deserves some happiness. You've heard the story about why I rented one of the apartments here."

"To keep an eye on Bobbi." Even after the librarian was acquitted of the murder of her husband a cloud of suspicion followed her. She took a different name and tried to change her life here in Carmel. But the mayor knew about her and wanted you to keep an eye on her. Bobbi was right. No matter what, some people would always believe that she deliberately killed her husband. Guilty with no chance for defense."

"It was that politically ambitious district attorney in Southern California," Bill said. "People like that don't think about others. Everything they do is for their own advancement. Ethics are not in their DNA. Bobbi's husband tried to kill her several times. The problem was proving it. Lucky she lived. Many times they don't."

"That's why I'm so worried about Laura. All her injuries…"

"Jaden, I know how you are. We will help Laura as much as we can. Right now I want you to forget about everything and get some sleep."

When he kissed her, she did forget about everything. The world vanished except for him.

He tucked the quilt around her shoulders and gently rubbed her temples until she relaxed. Tiredness washed over her. She no longer fought the darkness. Since she had been trapped in the cave, Jaden and the darkness carried on a running battle. Even the dank, sickening smell of the caves often came to her in darkness. At that time Jaden thought she was going to die alone. And no one would ever know what happened to her. How could she have been so stupid? Only because she had to find out what happened to Rosalba Bartlett more than a century earlier.

In the hospital Bill was so angry with her. Then he said he loved her. Bill stayed with her for days until she began to recover.by inches.

Finally, darkness descended like a mist. She welcomed a deep, dreamless sleep.

A sudden, brilliant light woke her. Jaden tried to move her feet first. They would not respond. Then she tried her arms. Slowly her right arm obeyed and she was able to push back the old wedding ring design quilt that her grandmother had made. This stiffness when she woke bothered her. *Makes me feel like I'm eighty years old.*

The doctor wanted her to go to physical therapy. Her excuse for not going was managing the shop. The cutlery shop, A Slice of Carmel, was time consuming 24/7. But this was her choice. She loved running the business. Her health was improving too slowly. Jaden's favorite times now were walks along Carmel Beach with Bill. When he had evening work shifts, she missed those pleasant times. *When he leaves, this apartment seems so empty. Like when you take down the Christmas tree. There is an empty space in the room.*

Several times Jaden thought he was going to propose. She wondered about her answer. After five years of being a widow the nagging thought was that she was being disloyal to Brent. They met in high school and were always best friends. With Bill it was different. She was drawn to him certainly not as a friend.

Jaden stumbled to the coffee maker. She smiled when she found Bill must have put in the coffee and water because it was all ready to go. Soon the aroma filled the apartment. Her arms and legs were working

When Jaden hung up she knew something was really wrong. She felt like she was breathing normally. For breakfast she microwaved oatmeal. This was her favorite breakfast with a spoonful of honey and two or three spoonfuls of yogurt plus milk. She often added fresh fruit.. *There could not be a healthier breakfast on the planet.*

Jaden enjoyed every mouthful. When she took her empty bowl to the sink, she noticed her answering machine was blinking. She pressed the button.

What she heard was so faint that she did not understand a word. Jaden pressed the button again and then the volume button. It was louder and garbled but this time she recognized the voice, the terrified voice. *Laura.* And the last word was "Help" that trailed off as she or someone else hung up. *Not again. Not again. The abused woman could not take another beating.*

Heart thumping, Jaden automatically dialed Bill's cell phone.

"Hi, Jaden."

She explained the message.

"You know it was Laura?"

"Bill, I'm positive, though she never said her name. She might have passed out."

"I'm driving so I'll go over to the shop right now. Where do they live?"

"In the apartment above the shop. Thanks. I'm really worried." Jaden tried to stop her hands from shaking. They would not cooperate.

"I'm in front right now. Be back in a minute. Hang on."

The minute dragged into what seemed like hours. Probably no more than four or five minutes.

Finally Bill's voice returned. "Jaden, the shop is closed. There is no noise or movement inside. I rang the buzzer and knocked on the door. I'm waiting to hear any sound, any response. Right now there is nothing else I can do."

Gloom surrounded her like a gray fog. "You can't go in?"

"Not without a better reason. A 911 call from here or something to indicate probable cause. There's nothing. I'm sorry."

"That's all right, I'll keep calling several times this morning."

She thought of breaking into the shop herself but decided against it. That would make a great headline for the local paper. Jaden Steele, local owner of A Slice of Carmel, arrested for breaking into the Village Gift Shop.

She would keep trying to call Laura. Where is Jeff? He must have done something to her. Or maybe there was nothing to it. She let her imagination run wild. But that distressed phone call was from Laura. Jaden played the message again. Although the voice was faint it blasted into Jaden's ears. When Laura called, she needed help. She was alive then. Jaden prayed that she was still alive. *I've got to get some sleep. It's only 8:30. Why am I so tired all the time?*

She went to the cupboard to find her multi-vitamins. Jaden took so many pills during her recovery that she was sick of them. Finally getting down to the multi-vitamin, calcium, and vitamin C only was a big step. No pain pills. Every once in a while she took an aspirin if she was really feeling lousy. A stressful day usually brought that on. Busy days used to make her happy. It meant the business was doing well. Now, they made her tired.

But she felt like she was getting better. Just much too slowly.

There was a knock on the door. Turned out to be Bobbi. Jaden told her as much as she knew had happened.

"Doesn't sound good." Bobbi put some half and half in her coffee. She loved coffee with half and half. Jaden never wanted to doctor her own brew with anything.

"I'm going by the gift store tomorrow," Bobbi stated. "If it's still closed, do you think a complaint from me would get the police to go in?"

"Not sure," Jaden took a sip of her coffee. "If only there were a good reason. The phone caller didn't identify herself. I know it was Laura."

"Let's think of something," Bobbi said, taking a huge sip of coffee.

"After two days that should be enough time to complain to Bill. Laura and Jeff live upstairs above the store. Laura never mentioned their going anywhere. She must still be there."

"I know something is wrong, Bobbi."

Bobbi nodded. She hugged Jaden. "We'll figure something out. Get some rest."

Sleep and the darkness usually were enemies for Jaden unless Bill was with her. He was tender and kind. She felt he was holding back, though, maybe because of her health. She always slept peacefully in his strong arms. Bill was working tonight or she would call him. Maybe she should have asked Bobbi to stay. Every two hours Jaden woke and paced the apartment until she became so sleepy that she returned to bed. That was only to repeat the process until the first rays of the sunrise. Jaden felt like going back to bed. Her head ached from so much interrupted sleep. Feeling helpless made her shaky. Maybe some coffee would help.

Jaden yawned. "I have to get myself ready and open the shop." She would rather stay in bed. "Move, legs," she mumbled.

After she dressed in gray slacks and a white sleeveless blouse, Jaden put on her black cotton jacket. Her hand went to the Monarch knife in her pocket. Her late husband had the torsion blade knife made especially for her hand. She rarely left it home. Some people had good luck charms. She had Brent's gift, the Monarch.

The customer traffic into A Slice of Carmel was slow. Only two people since she opened at ten. This gave her time to dust, clean the glass windows, and straighten the displays. Ruth's orchid in the display window really set off the arrangement.

"I'd better give you a little water. Ruth always said 'Don't overwater. A little once a week is fine.' "

When Jaden was in the bathroom getting some water, the front door bell jangled. She came out with the water which she almost dropped. Jaden used her left hand to prop up her shaking right hand holding the glass. Jeff was standing inside in front of the glass door.

"Mornin'." He took a step forward.

Jaden caught a whiff of alcohol. Heavy drinkers don't realize that alcohol oozes out of their pores. They sometimes try to cover their breath with a mint or gum. With Jeff this was like dumping a glass of water in the ocean. An alcohol cloud came out of his mouth with the *Mornin'*. She wanted to escape. The only other exit was the emergency one window upstairs.

"Can I help you?" Jaden tried to cover her surprise and nervousness by slowly pouring water into the orchid. He came up behind her. She turned, placing the glass on the display counter.

"Yeah."

Another strong whiff of alcohol wafted into her face with his one word. Jaden thought, *It's only eleven a.m. His nose is red but he's no Santa Claus.*

"Yeah. You know where my wife is?"

"What?"

"Laura's gone."

"When did she leave?" Jaden's heart was suddenly drumming louder than her voice, so she barely heard herself.

"Last night, I think. I can't remember. I found your card and that Bobbi librarian's card in my wife's purse."

No woman is going away for a day without her purse. *Laura's dead and he probably killed her. He's a real alcoholic who no doubt has blackouts.* Her stomach cramped so much that it hurt.

"I don't know where she is. Think. Did you do something to her?" She heard the nervous tremor in her voice.

"I don't . . . know. There was some blood." The words slurred.

Oh, God. No. "She's hurt?"

"She's clumsy. Thinned skin. Any little bump she bleeds all over the place."

Jaden's drumming heart skipped some beats. "She might be at the hospital. I'll call."

"You know where she is! You're going to warn her!" He suddenly grabbed Jaden's left arm.

Her right hand flew into her pocket and she touched the spring of the torsion blade. She brought the open knife up to his neck in about three seconds.

"You let go of me, you bastard, or you won't live another second. We'll see how thin skinned you are. Jeff's red rimmed eyes widened. He lifted both hands high.

"Hey. Hey. Don't cut me. I'm leaving. I'm leaving. Right now."

He backed up so quickly that he slammed into the glass entry door. The bell flew off the door handle, hitting the floor with a distressed clang.

Jaden thought of holding him while she called Bill. How long can the response to a 911 call be?

How long could she hold him? Her heart was racing. She was breathing in gasps. Finding Jeff in Carmel in his condition would certainly not be a problem for the police.

Jeff yanked open the door to dash outside. His first few steps he stumbled. Jaden tossed her knife so that it stuck into the door frame. Smiling, she calmly walked over and pulled it out, closed the blade, and dropped it back into her pocket. With her free left hand she closed and locked the door.

Jaden had been so quick about pulling the knife because she had practiced the move a hundred times. Many of her hours in the shop, Jaden was alone. If a robber came in, he could take all the money or all the knives. In today's world the epidemic like the plague was dangerous. Drug abuse was another plague. Who knows what a person on meth or another dangerous drug would do? The most valuable thing in the shop was her life. Monarch was insurance. She could at least fight back. Brent had taught her any number of self-defense moves. Bill knew about the knife. He never said a word.

A sudden wave of dizziness hit her. Trembling, Jaden sank down on her desk chair. *What if he had called her bluff? What then?* She was still proud of herself. Confronting a killer never occurred to her when she was drinking her morning coffee. Bullies like Jeff always picked on the helpless. If someone confronted them, they did not know what to do because they were cowards at heart. They worked in the dark or behind masks. Jaden would probably wonder forever what she would have done if he had not backed down.

This has to be enough to get a search warrant for the shop and the living quarters.
She went to her desk to call Bill. He was in the shop in a few minutes.

"I'm going to kill him," Bill muttered. "If you had done it, I would not even have arrested you."

"He said there was blood in their living quarters. Can you get a search warrant? And no woman leaves without her purse. She's probably in there dead. I should have done more to help her."

"You did your best. So did Bobbi. These are the worst situations. I will ask my captain right away for a warrant. Plenty of cause now."

"That will take time. She might still be alive, but hurt."

"Maybe not. I promise you that we will be in the shop this afternoon. We can get in with what you've told me or even if I have to say that I heard someone yelling for help."

When she was recovering from being trapped in the caves, Jaden finally gave up all pretense of being an independent woman. Her fear of Bill was gone. Life without him was unimaginable. If he asked her to marry him...*Yes or no?* Her marriage with Brent was ideal and fun. *Comfortable.* They had been friends since high school.

Making up her mind about marrying Bill seemed an impossible task.

Her friend, Bobbi, would marry David Bartlett in a minute. Jaden felt envious of her friend's obvious love for him. Bobbi did deserve happiness.

After everything the woman had been through, life on the remote estate was probably very appealing to her. And whenever she was around David, Bobbi actually glowed. They were in love! Before Bobbi tried to hide herself in Carmel Village her life was impossible. She had been on trial, accused of murdering her husband.

To Jaden the Bartlett estate was like the end of the world. It was where she almost died. And remote was not the best word. End of the world was a perfect description..

The only reason she would ever return would be for Bobbi. Jaden knew the estate was beautiful yet haunted. Maybe the ghosts, good and bad, would finally find their rest when love returned to the home of the long dead Captain Josiah Bartlett.

"Jaden, I'll let you know as soon as I can."

When he left, it crossed Jaden's mind to call Hal Lamont, the former owner of A Slice of Carmel and the owner of this complex of shops with their six apartments above. Then she decided she was all right by herself. The visit from Bill was enough to calm her. She went back to the computer to check on online orders. Those were a bigger and bigger part of her business. She thought some people today probably did all their shopping online. Saved driving. People liked that. It really hurt the physical shops, though.

I'll have to reorder some inventory. Need to thoroughly check the knife inventory. Not today.

The phone rang. Bill's voice sounded breathless, "I have permission to go in. Will let you know what happens but not for a while. Hang in there. First I will try to see if there is anyone who can answer the door. The warrant's coming so I can go right in."

After he hung up, she listened to the dial tone for a while. A sense of doom surrounded her. After she placed the phone in its cradle, Jaden sat down and continued to stare at it. *Please let Laura be all right.* She could not shake the bad vibes that now seemed to fill the shop.

"Jaden, I'll let you know as soon as I can. I promise. Try to be patient."

After he hung up, she stared at the desk top for a while. A sense of doom surrounded her. She could think of nothing but her failure to save Laura. Jaden sat down and continued to stare at the door. *Please let Laura be all right.* While she forced herself to keep busy, the waiting made the day progress in slow motion. Only an hour had gone by. It seemed like ten. She was distracted waiting and worrying. Jaden did the store's eternal paperwork much more slowly than normal.

Several shoppers came into the store and she made four good sales. Normally, this would have made her happy, while bustling showing the stock.

Her usual self would have been a good salesperson and maybe sold them more.

Today she could not keep Laura off her mind. And she played the incident with Jeff over and over. No regrets about that at all. Laura deserved better than him. She swallowed hard.

When the phone finally rang, she jumped for it. "Slice of Carmel. How can I help you?"

"Jaden, it's me." Bill cleared his throat.

"Did you find Laura?"

"No, Jaden, honey, I'm sorry...."

"What is it?"

"There's dried blood in the upstairs apartment. I've called in a forensic team from Monterey. We don't have one."

"But where is she?"

"She's not here. Jeff was so drunk he's still in a stupor. I can't get anything sensible out of him. He's going to be arrested. I'm sorry. It looks bad even if we can't find her."

Jaden muttered, "Oh, no."

"Right now it looks like he might have taken her somewhere, probably the ocean, and dropped her in. God knows there's plenty of places in Big Sur where she would never be found. Along the cliffs into the ocean or in the woods."

Jaden felt sick to her stomach. Blood. *Laura didn't take her purse.* She fought the idea of telling Bobbi because then both of them would be upset.

"I'll wait until Bill tells me more." The news would roll through the Village like a morning mist. They maybe had until morning before the news would be everywhere in town and probably the evening news.

A normal news day in town might be the arrest of a shoplifter. The disappearance of a local shop owner under mysterious circumstances would be headlines way beyond Carmel-by-the-Sea. *Why did Laura have to stay with that monster alcoholic husband?* She tried to understand. Why didn't the woman listen?

He might have killed her when he was drunk, but making her disappear...he could not have done that as a fumbling alcoholic. But Laura was so petite. She felt certain he could have easily dragged her to the car.

The temptation to call Bill again overwhelmed her. Except he was busy right now. Patience. She knew he would tell her everything later. Jaden sat down at her desk and put her head in her hands. Her eyes were moist with tears. After about twenty minutes she took a tissue to wipe her eyes and blow her nose. Is there anything I can do now? Was there anything else I could have done for Laura to convince her to get out of there?

The phone rang again. She grabbed it so quickly she almost knocked it off the desk. She caught it halfway down.

"A Slice of Carmel." She answered, fumbled with the phone until it was on its proper place. On the desk.

"Jaden, I'm at the station. We've arrested Jeff and are waiting for him to be assigned an attorney. He hasn't one and no money to pay for one."

"Has he said anything about Laura?"

"Jeff Just keeps repeating that he does not know where she is."

"He just doesn't remember." She heard her voice rising.

"A reporter from the Monterey news is already on the way over here. You should call Bobbi before she hears some other way."

Jaden hated to disturb Bobbi at work, but knew this was important. Bobbi was actually one of the last people to talk to Laura....alive. Her throat constricted. The first words to Bobbi came out as a frog-like croak. After gulping a swallow of water, she asked, "Are you in the middle of something really important?"

"What's happened? Go ahead. There's no one at the desk right now."

"Bobbi, I won't go over the details.. Jeff came in the store, drunk and belligerent, looking for Laura. He insisted Laura was gone. But her purse with her wallet and our cards was in the cupboard above the sink. He rambled on about blood. I called Bill and he got a search warrant. Jeff was there passed out. According to Bill there was blood in the bedroom and bathroom, but no Laura. If they don't keep Jeff in custody, he has your home information, too. I don't think he can get out for two days. The story will be in the papers and on tv by tomorrow."

"Thanks for telling me, Jaden. I feel sick that we could not have helped Laura. I even saw myself in her situation. All I felt was a black future. Like I knew what was coming. Like I was reliving my nightmare trial."

"You did the best you could at the time. I feel the same way. Do you think I could have done something else for Laura?"

"Not until she decided to do something for herself. Laura was too beat down. I knew just how she felt. I was faster in wanting to get out of the trap. Some of the abusers, I'm afraid most of them, never give up. I think their whole life depends on dominating someone. It sounds like we were trying too late. I feel sick about Laura."

"Me, too."

"Jeff made sure she did not have any friends. I didn't ask Bill if her cell phone was in her purse. If it is, that would make me lose hope for Laura."

"You're right. My husband found fault with all of my friends. If I would mention a name he would have something bad to say about them. He kept wearing me down. He kept me isolated with no friends. Finally they stopped calling."

Of course. That would give them almost absolute power over the weaker partner. A possessive domination. Exactly like being a prisoner.

Until the incident with Jeff today, Jaden had had a difficult time believing that abusers existed. Then she saw how Jeff thought he could intimidate her like he did with Laura. What a cowardly bully.

"Bobbi, I'll call you again as soon as I hear more. Would you like to have dinner?"

"David's coming. We would love you to come with us. We'll probably go out to the wharf. Hopefully we can relax a little."

Jaden smiled when she caught the brightness in Bobbi's voice. "I'll call you with anything new. I'm still praying that Laura is all right."

"I will."

If Bobbi moved to Big Sur, it was not really too far away. She understood why her friend would be attracted by the safety of the remote estate and its handsome owner.

Her thoughts jumped back to the current situation. The chance for Laura to be alive was slim, but not impossible.

There is always some hope. Those were her grandmother's words. Jaden remembered them when she was trapped under the Bartlett house in Big Sur. The acrid smell of the rats made her sick. When the skeleton of a rabbit stared at her in the last beam of her flashlight before the battery died, Jaden grasped at the hope of finding her way out as the rabbit had found its way in. Weak as she was, Jaden braced herself against the slimy rock wall, going forward, forward, until a beam of light hurt her swollen eyes. *Freedom. The light meant freedom.*

Right now she felt as though she had more hope then than they did now of finding Laura alive.

Who leaves without her wallet and phone? And that worthless husband was capable of anything once he started drinking, which appeared to be a constant addiction.

Jaden's head was aching. "It's lunchtime and I certainly could use some coffee. I'm probably having withdrawal symptoms." A cup of the Mad Hatter's coffee would be great. The best coffee in Carmel was right next door at the coffee shop. She turned the sign on the door to *Closed*, got her phone and purse, and locked the shop door.

"Super clam chowder and coffee?" Kyle asked as she sat down at one of the outdoor tables in their sunny court.

"Nice that I don't even have to ask."

"But, dear, if you don't mind my saying, did you get enough sleep last night?"

"Do I look that bad?"

"To me you always look lovely. Just today you look tired and lovely. Is it your police friend?"

The Edge of Carmel

Gossip was Kyle's middle name. But he was never mean spirited and was a superior listener. He never interrupted with his own views on the problem unless asked.

He poured coffee into her mug. Jaden took a deep breath and relaxed in the outdoor chair. The unusually loud sound of ocean waves filled the air, drowning out the noise of the constant traffic and the tourists who filled the sidewalks. Strange how some days the ocean was whisper quiet. It has people-like moods. Her mind and body were relaxing too much. She was almost afraid she would fall asleep right here. She took another deep breath to relax.

Kyle returned with the steaming chowder. Chef Sydney made the best in Carmel. Jaden often bought a quart and sourdough bread for dinner. Kyle and

Sydney owned and ran the café. Sydney graduated from a culinary academy. Jaden could not remember which one. He must have been their star pupil.

"Thank you. You are an angel to always remember what I like. What a morning." The news would be out soon anyway. She told him about the morning's unnerving events.

He sat down in the chair opposite her. "That is quite a story. No wonder you look tired. I'd better keep an eye on who comes into your store. Sounds like you can handle yourself but there are some real nut jobs wandering around in today's world. Do you think Laura was murdered? You're right. She would not leave without her purse or at least her wallet. When do you think you will hear more from Bill?"

"No way of knowing. Oh, this chowder is heavenly. Please compliment Sydney." She sipped another creamy spoonful. "If only we could have done more for Laura."

"The woman had to do something for herself. You were trying. You can't force people to change their behavior overnight."

"Kyle, if she is dead, I am going to feel responsible forever."

He rose because a young couple sat down at one of the outdoor tables. "Don't do that to yourself, Jaden. You can't cure the world. If you can improve your little part of the planet, that's all you can do. You tried. Bobbi tried."

The warm sun, coffee, and chowder relaxed her so that she almost felt normal. He was right. Was Bill ever going to call? She fought the temptation to pull out her phone.

Since people were coming in for lunch she decided to open the shop because some of them would browse the store before they left the court. A chance for a sale was important to the month's receipts. She knew that the closed Village Gift shop was not making sales. The Jeff she saw was not capable of handling any business. She guessed that Laura probably did everything related to the shop and was abused for her trouble. And she was cut off from having friends. What a terrible life. Bobbi said that was typical. The abuser has something bad to say about everyone, even family members, so that you feel isolated. "You desperately want to please him." Bobbi told her, "You can't. No matter how hard you try, you can't."

Back in the store, Jaden opened her computer to check on orders. There was one. One of their best knives. $599 plus shipping. To Connecticut of all places. Don't they have cutlery stores in the East? No tax since the knife was going out of state. This was a testament to the internet. No wonder so many physical stores have a difficult time staying in business. No need for a physical store and a lease to pay. She found the knife, the packing materials, and a mailing box. Before Jaden closed the box, she printed out a packing slip. The customer had paid by credit card online. She could close the store for enough time to go to the post office which was only a block away. Good exercise walking there every day. Carmel was unique because there were no street addresses. Everyone had a post office box. Jaden wondered how the building could hold enough boxes for all the village residents..

And how do emergency crews find a house with no address?

She leapt for the phone when it rang. This time it was Bobbi, "Hi, Jaden. Any news about Laura?"

"No. I've been waiting to hear from Bill. Nothing but silence."

"Do you want to go to dinner with us? Bill, too, if he's not working. Nice to get together, even under the circumstances."

"I think it would be good to go out. I'll phone Bill. Been waiting for him to call with any news but there must be nothing new. And he is busy with paperwork, I'm sure."

"We'll go out to the wharf. The ocean is relaxing. Unless there is a storm."

"I like it even when it is stormy. That sounds wonderful. I'll let you know as soon as I can."

She left a message for Bill.

When he finally called, Bill's normally strong voice sounded thready. Jaden knew he must be tired.

"Do you feel like going out?" she asked. "David is coming to take Bobbi to dinner and they have invited us."

"I think that would be really a good diversion for you."

"Is there any news about Laura?"

"No, but we've found some disturbing information on Jeff's computer."

After she hung up, Jaden wondered what could be on Jeff's computer. *He can't be any computer expert in his condition. Maybe it's porn. Some of that is so vile she could imagine that it might be incriminating. Viewing could explain some of his cruel behavior. Maybe act as a trigger?*

As much as she tried to push the thoughts away, she couldn't keep Laura out of her mind.

Going out would distract her. Jaden called Bobbi to set up a dinner time at seven.

The Edge of Carmel

By the time she showered and changed to her blue cotton dress, Jaden felt like climbing into bed, dressed or not, and taking another nap. Her sleeveless dress had a long sleeved jacket that made it perfect for every occasion. The dress was like a faithful old friend that everyone had seen many times. Someday, she told herself, she would go over to Monterey to go clothes shopping. The time never seemed to arrive. Her eighty-three year old neighbor, Esther, often said that time was the most precious gift. Jaden thought it was because of her age, but now she realized how right Esther was.

Jaden fastened the necklace with the silver, heart shaped locket that Bill had given her for Christmas. She loved the locket and loved him. Several times she thought he was going to ask her to marry him. What would she say? For that commitment she knew she must put Brent into a closet of memories.

Because her outfit was pocketless, Jaden slipped her Monarch into her evening bag. Since they all lived in the apartments upstairs over the Dolores Court shops, Bobbi and David and Bill were coming together to get her. Esther Stennis and her son lived in one apartment, Kyle and Sydney the fifth, and the mysterious Emile Von Otto in the last apartment. Jaden had never met him and neither had anyone else. Every once in a while he was there because the trash barrel mysteriously filled. He drifted in and out like a ghost several times a year. She thought he was either very strange or very rude to have never introduced himself to anyone in Dolores Street Court.

When the bell rang, she called "Come in, Bobbi and David, please."

David entered first and hugged her. "You look great, Jaden." Of course this was his first view of Old Faithful Blue Dress. Bobbi and Bill might be tired of it. Bobbi looked sensational in a black skirt and a black and gold silk top with three quarter length sleeves. The gold reflected what looked like gold flecks in her almond shaped hazel eyes.

Jaden made a mental note to ask Bobbi to come with her on the "some day" shopping trip. But to be honest, Bobbi was one of those women who would look good in an old-fashioned flour sack dress or anything else she wore. They walked down to the parking garage. David opened the back door of his Highlander for the women. Bill sat in the front seat.

As they moved out of the garage, Jaden was thinking about how her grandmother told her they actually made dresses for children out of flour sacks.

You would lie on the white sack and mom would draw the outline of your body. Then Grandma would sew over the lines and cut off the extra sacking. There was your dress. They did not waste much in the old days.. Some of the sacking scraps went to the outhouse. She smiled at the thought.

Jaden wondered how many children today would wear a flower sack dress. And/ orr who would buy a twenty-five or fifty pound bag of flour? Her grandmother.   A baker? No, they must buy big barrels of flour.

"You have a beautiful smile," David, an eternal charmer, complimented. "I saw a glimpse of you smiling at the car window."

"I was daydreaming," she admitted. "Good memories about my grandmother. Funny how these snatches of memory come back for no reason at all."

"Your grandparents raised you," David responded. "They are important memories."

"What were you thinking?" Bill asked.

"Oh, my grandmother bought flour in fifty pound sacks. She used the flour to make pancakes, biscuits, bread, cookies—all from scratch. I was thinking how few people today would do that." Half of her thoughts were enough explanation. She did not want to say that she felt a little like Cinderella next to the Princess Bobbi. Or maybe they looked like princess and the pauper. The librarian was her best friend. When Jaden moved from her home in Nebraska, she left all of her childhood friends behind. In Carmel she made friends very quickly. She felt lucky since all of her family was gone.

"Why were you thinking about your grandmother's baking?" Bill touched her arm lightly. The small gesture made her want to reach out to him. She resisted.

"The memories sometimes come out of nowhere like that. Trying to go back to a pleasant time. I can almost smell her bread baking. The best smell in the world. I stayed in the kitchen until the bread came out of the oven so I could have the first hot bite. Funny what one remembers."

"I get flashes like that," Bobbi admitted. "Usually it's my mother saying something like

Have you brushed your teeth, Roberta? Brush them every night."

They all laughed.

"Jaden leaned back in the seat and sighed. This had already worked. Her memories pushed the thought of poor Laura out of her mind.

The lights from the boats docked at Monterey Harbor reflected on the dark water. The Clamshell was Jaden's favorite restaurant because of the view of the water. Harbor sea lions were an extra bonus during the day, like dinner theater. Tonight they were resting, crowded together right above the water on one of the docks below.

The Edge of Carmel

The distraction of this evening out in the company of good friends was just what she needed. The waiter, Ricardo, impressed her friends by immediately bringing Jaden her favorite Riesling. The others ordered the evening's special, scampi. Jaden was tempted but finally decided on her favorite, calamari.

"The waiter knows you. How often do you come here?" Bobbi asked with a smile.

"Ricardo has a phenomenal memory. Next time you come he will remember your names. It's a great skill for a waiter."

"Or anyone else," Bobbi commented. "I remember most of our library regulars but that's because they come in all the time."

Jaden relaxed as she sipped her wine. "I understand. Our regular store customers are no problem. Sometimes a face will look familiar, but the name will escape me. That's when I smile and hope I will get a hint quickly. So many of our clients are regulars. Every once in a while someone, I call them the unforgettable, comes in the door and I wish I could disappear into the upstairs apartment. No matter what, they will never be happy. Our Hal is really good at handling those people."

"He's had about forty years of experience," Bobbi told her. "A few people are not easy to deal with no matter how patient you are. Even when you agree with them, they are angry."

They all laughed again. Jaden imagined David was hermiting at his remote estate in Big Sur. He obviously was not anxious to deal with most people. She and Bobbi dealt with the difficult ones sometimes. Very rare, but those types you always remembered. In her store life she knew that ninety-five percent of people were great. The remaining percenters she would gladly drop in the Carmel River. With luck they could get washed out to sea.

She felt herself relaxing at that thought. Along with the company and the good food, were the lights on the water. With Bill beside her, Jaden knew she was loved. He made her feel safe. Being with Bobbi and David made her push the apprehension about Laura to the back of her mind.

David changed the subject, "Is there any more news you can tell us about the missing woman? I know Bobbi and Jaden are really worried."

"No," Bill answered. "Nothing. We did learn something from Jeff's computer, though, about a completely different case that we have been investigating for the last eight months. Do you know about the threatening emails that some of the city council members have been receiving? The technicians we used could not trace the emails for some reason. I should not talk but you can guess."

Jaden immediately jumped in, "They were on Jeff's computer?"

"I did not exactly tell you that. It really shows that he has some mental problems. Jeff is dangerous. If you see him, please call 911 right away."

"I'd believe anything about him," Jaden added. "Dangerous coward."

"The emails were meant to intimidate whoever read them." Bill took a bite of his scampi. "People with a lot of repressed anger use the net to bully others. I think that they try to build themselves up that way instead of forging their own path."

Jaden saw Bobbi turn in her chair to face the large picture window next to their table. She wiped her eyes with her napkin. *This is upsetting her. I'll change the subject.*

"Have you seen Frederic Melnicoff lately?" Jaden asked Bobbi. She did not understand why that question popped into her mind. The Russian ballet star usually contacted Jaden once a month to tell her how his Pacific Grove café was doing or update her on his American citizenship application. Both she and Bobbi had dated him. Nothing ever serious.

At any gathering a crowd of women would surround him. As a world famous ballet star he had a right to a world class ego, but he was gracious and always interested in what she was doing. For a relationship he would have to be shared with too many other admirers. The well -known dancer toured often with his newly formed Golden State Ballet Company.

When dinner was over, Jaden hesitated to leave the warm restaurant and the pleasant company.

"That dinner was just what I needed," Jaden told her three companions at the front door of the apartment. Bill came in and waited until she got ready for bed. He did not stay after he pulled the covers over her shoulders and kissed her gently.

"Good night," he said quietly.

"The night was wonderful, Bill,"

Jaden regretted that he left. She did feel almost completely relaxed, because in one corner of her mind, she saw pale faced Laura. Her eyes were open, staring straight ahead. The dead white of her skin frightened Jaden into thinking the worst. Finally, she mercifully fell into a deep, dreamless sleep.

The phone woke her at seven-thirty. Good thing. She might have slept through the time to open the store.

"Good morning," she mumbled into the phone's receiver.

"Jaden?" A thin older voice asked.

It was Ruth.

"Yes. Ruth, is that you? You sound weak. Are you sick?"

"Not really. Jaden, I wondered if you could come to lunch today or tomorrow?"

She had been to Ruth's house before to pick up orchids when Ruth was sick. The back of her house was perched on long metal piers at the end of a cul-de-sac on the edge of Carmel next to Monterey. Jaden sometimes helped when she was not well by making her deliveries to customers in the village.

The older woman's voice had reminded her of when Ruth was sick. It meant trouble, but she answered,

"I'll be glad to. Today is fine. The store is quiet this morning and it's only five minutes to your place if I drive. An easy walk but that would take another 20-25 minutes."

"Oh, the sooner the better would be good." Her voice sounded brighter.

"I'll come at twelve, maybe a little after, if that's all right with you."

"Will be expecting you," Ruth answered. "Jaden, thank you so much. You are an angel. I have a problem that I can't solve myself. I do need help."

Jaden wondered what kind of a problem Ruth could possibly have. Money? Jaden knew she was low income but had never at any time complained about money. She could be sick again. The last time Jaden saw her she felt that Ruth was looking more fragile than normal.

Had Ruth almost said, "*We'll* be expecting you?" She passed the thought off as part of her very active imagination.

The day was a slow one that dragged. Busy days are so much more fun, she thought. Slow days made her yawn.

Only three customers came in the store all morning. She found herself typically yawning. The fresh air would be welcome. She sometimes walked down to the beach on her lunch hour. If Bobbi was free, she would stop by and they both would walk to the beach or window shop in the many stores and galleries that drew thousands of tourists to the area every year.

When Bobbi and David were married, she would miss her friend so much. She could see how happy the two were together. Bobbi smiled and was more animated when she was with David Bartlett. After the trauma of her life, Bobbi deserved happiness. While Jaden found his remote Big Sur estate lonely, Bobbi thought of it as a perfect place to live "away from the madding crowd."

She knew that Frederick was interested in Bobbi. Although he was a charming person nothing ever jelled between them.

Frederick could have his pick of women. At any gathering they both attended, a crowd of women would surround him. She might as well not be there.

As a world famous ballet star he had every right to a world class ego, but he was always gracious and interested in what you were doing. If Bill were not in the picture, she could be very interested in Frederick.

"I would have to share him with too many admirers," she told herself the obvious about attractive celebrities.

One of Jaden's life rules was that *Things always change*. And Bobbi at least once a week would ask her about Bill. To be honest, Jaden could not imagine life without him. Her happy life with her late husband, Brent, was fading in her memory. Sometimes she had to look at his picture to recall his face. For a long time she felt that she was being disloyal to him if she dated. Meeting Sergio Manetti changed all that. She had thought he might be the one to replace Brent.

That was probably the hundredth time Jaden had gone over how foolish she had been. There is no way to change the past. Slowly, she understood that Brent would want her to go on with her life.

Bill made her happy.

Jaden turned the door sign to *Closed*. Be back at 1:30. She locked the door but did not turn on the alarm because she knew that Kyle would be watching the store. She walked down the concrete steps to the parking garage for tenants of the court.

She started her old Toyota Camry and headed out on 6th Street. Since the car had 150,068 miles, Jaden often wondered if or when she might have to buy another one. Bobbi told her not to worry as she felt sure it would last to 300,000 miles. She turned the car on Junipero and took a couple of turns onto Carpenter St. Less traffic to the freeway on Carpenter. You could see the back of Ruth's house from the freeway. Tall supporting piers went from the back of the houses way down into the hillside. She turned on Seabreeze Court and drove to the end of the cul-de-sac. Ruth's house looked deserted. The orchid lady did not own a car. Usually a friend brought her and her orchids into Carmel.

Jaden set the brake and stepped out onto the black slate sidewalk that led to the front door. An offshoot led around the corner to a side door. She walked straight to the front door. When Jaden pressed the door chime she was surprised to find that the door opened almost immediately. Ruth greeted her, "Come right in." As soon as Jaden stepped in a pale faced Ruth closed the door behind her.

"Come into the dining room, Jaden. Lunch is very simple soup and sandwiches. Thanks so much for coming. It's so that we tell you."

"What is it, Ruth?" She gasped when she looked at the dining table. Laura was sitting there. She looked even paler than Ruth. Her right eye was black and swollen. The whole side of her face looked misshapen. Jaden winced at the thought of how much it must hurt.

"Laura!" The combination of surprise at seeing her and relief that she was alive made Jaden cry out.

She grabbed for a chair to steady herself. "Laura, I'm so glad that you are…." Jaden ran over to hug her. Laura sighed. She trembled. She was hurting. Jaden checked herself from saying "alive." How did the woman get here? Why had she and Ruth not reported that she was alive?

"Would you like iced tea or coffee?" Ruth asked, ignoring Jaden's surprised outburst. "Sugar? Milk?"

Jaden gulped out, "Black coffee, Ruth." She sat down next to Laura. Jaden touched her arm lightly to make certain the woman was real, that this was not a dream. Laura flinched. Her arm was yellowed in spots, like old bruises were healing.

Ruth poured her a steaming cup. "Laura," Jaden finally was able to ask, "Laura, Ruth, everyone is so worried. The police are looking for you."

"I know." Ruth sat down. "That's why I called. Jeff has been arrested. He's a murder suspect, but Laura is alive."

"What happened?"

Ruth passed her a plate of sandwiches. Jaden chose a tuna. Ruth doctored the tuna with sweet pickles and cilantro, not mayo, but something she could not quite identify. She composed herself enough to say, "This is delicious. What is the dressing?" The older woman answered, "Blue cheese dressing and a spoonful of salsa."

"I never would have guessed, but what a wonderful combination." Babbling about the dressing must be from the shock and relief of seeing Laura alive.

"Thanks, Jaden. Laura is going to tell you what happened. That will explain why we did not call the police right away."

Laura began, "We are afraid, Jaden. We need advice on what to do."

Of course they are afraid of Jeff.

Jaden reached out for Laura's hand. "It's all right, whatever you tell me."

"I was getting ready for bed when Jeff came home. It was eight o'clock so I had assumed he had eaten. I could smell he had been drinking. He's always drinking...." Her face turned red and tears filled her eyes.

Ruth handed her a Kleenex. "It's all right, dear. You are safe."

Laura cleared her throat. "He started yelling that there was no dinner. I tried to get into the kitchen to warm something up, but he grabbed my arm and squeezed until it hurt.

I said 'Just be a few minutes. The television dinner just takes a few minutes.'"

Laura's hands started to tremble, "'Too late!' he yelled and hit me on the side of my head. I fell down. Tried to pretend I was unconscious, but he yanked me back up and shoved me against the counter. He hit me across the side of the face again. I don't remember anything after that. When I woke up, what felt like needles were burning everywhere inside of me. Moving made me cry. I heard snoring.

He was in a kitchen chair, snoring away. I stared at him for a few seconds. It was like I saw him for the first time. He was a mean, disgusting bully.

*I'm leaving, e*xploded in my mind.

When I pulled myself up, my whole body was like little jabs of sparking electricity. I wanted to die, but forced myself out of the kitchen area to the bathroom for a towel to press on the bleeding. My silk scarf was hanging on the door. I grabbed it to put over my head. I was clinging to the railing down the stairs, not certain if I could walk. I finally got out of the building. I was crying from the pain and could only see out of my left eye. My right eye was swollen shut. My face. was throbbing. What I decided was that I was never going back to any place where Jeff could hurt me. Nothing was my fault. Well, staying for so long was my fault. I did not care if I ever saw him again. He could kill me without even knowing it. I walked out of town on Carpenter Street. Could not stop sobbing. I had nothing except the clothes I was wearing. Walked up to Highway One, but, of course could not cross. My body started trembling. My legs were wobbling as I collapsed to the path. Passed out for I don't know how long. When I woke up the sun was gone. My vision was so blurry I could not tell if it was an evening mist or a veil of tears. Something came to me through the watery haze--.the rear of the houses that were along my side of the freeway. The houses were supported on metal pillars at least twenty feet high, but there was a foot path that led along the freeway up the hill to the beginning of Seabreeze Court.

Stumbled up there and remembered that the house at the end of the street was Ruth's. Once I took her some orchids that had lost their blooms. Needed to tell her we did not want the orchids anymore because we were trying to cut expenses."

Ruth said, "When I opened the door she collapsed against me. I managed to get her to bed. I nursed her injuries as well as I could. She begged me not to tell anyone because she was terrified that Jeff would come after her. I wanted to take her to emergency but understood the danger if he found out where she was. I don't have a car so would have needed to call a friend. They would have asked about her injuries."

Jaden offered, "She was right about the danger. Jeff is a malicious bully."

Ruth poured herself a glass of iced tea. "Laura could not move for two days. When she woke up she did nothing but cry, begged me not to call a doctor or tell anyone else where she was. I knew she was right about Jeff. He would never let her escape. Lucky she got away from him before...."

Ruth did not finish but Jaden completed the sentence in her own mind. This was the worst type of case, according to Bill. Women were often trapped or could see no way out. A good percentage died. Jaden's stomach knotted. Laura was safe at the moment. If Jeff learned where she was it would be a nightmare. Lucky he was in jail.

"What we need to do is to notify the police that Laura is all right," Ruth said.

"Please, Jaden, please, I don't want Jeff to know where I am. Please."

"I'll ask Bill what to do. Laura should be photographed by the police, though. It's been a few days, but that's important." Jaden knew how important pictures of Laura would be if there were a trial. She should take some with her own phone.

"Thanks, Jaden," Ruth said.

"I'll let you know what Bill says as soon as I can." She stood up. "Can I take some pictures, Laura? They will be very important for you."

"All right," Laura answered, eyes looking downward. Jaden fought back the tears as she took the photos. How could anyone do this to another person? Her hands were shaking when she took several pictures. The injuries made her stomach knot.

She felt overwhelmed with gratitude that Laura was still alive. That alone was a miracle. It made her sick to her stomach to realize that when this news came out Jeff would probably be out of jail. There was no way to watch him every minute. The pattern for people like this was that they would dedicate themselves to following and probably terrorizing, sometimes killing their victim. A fixation. Any way Jaden thought about this situation, it was impossible.

She needed to ask Bill, but already guessed that this news could not be kept quiet. The knot in her stomach turned into a granite rock.

Laura sighed deeply and finally said, "Jaden, I could not stand hurting all the time." Her face turned red. "I could not stay. I won't go back."

Jaden hugged her. She was trembling. "You won't have to go back. Ever!"

Ruth came over, "Laura, would you like to go back to bed?"

Laura nodded. They walked with her to the bedroom closest to the stairway that led to the basement floor. Ruth's pickle barrels and a separate sink were down there. No one was ever asked into the "below."

"They might steal my secret spice recipe," Ruth insisted. The house was three stories. Jaden wondered how Ruth was handling the stairs now. Jaden noticed that she was walking with more effort every time she came to visit the shop. Her complexion, unusually smooth for someone of her age, was turning paler and paler. *No one can escape time,* Jaden remembered her eighty-three year old neighbor, Esther Stennis, saying *Do the best you can with the time you have. No one is guaranteed any tomorrow. Don't waste your time.*

"Laura, get some rest now. I promise you no one will make you go back. No one."

When the door closed, Jaden and Ruth went back to have a cup of coffee.

"I heard this noise in the middle of the night." Ruth poured them steaming coffee. "First, I was going to call 911, but then I heard her voice. I recognized her although it was a terrified cry. Took a deep breath and opened the door. Jaden, she was bleeding from a cut on her face and her teeth were bloody. She collapsed into my arms. I barely got her to the bed. Then I realized how many people would know if I called emergency. As I told you she begged me not to or not to take her to a doctor because that monster husband of hers would know where she was. Every time I touched her trying to clean the wounds and put on antiseptic, she cried. I had some antibiotic lotion and some oral antibiotics that I gave her, plus sleeping pills. She slept for twenty hours. I would have let that man rot in jail, but knew we would have to admit she was alive. He's lucky she is. I don't know how Laura has stood this abuse for so long."

"At least she has finally had enough. We just have to find out how to tell the police and keep her away from him. I'll talk to Bill first. He can suggest something."

"All right. But I am not going to let that monster near her. Ever! No matter what."

"You would not be any match for a mean bully like Jeff."

"You would be surprised what one can do if it becomes necessary." Her words came in a robot like monotone. Ruth stood up but did not move for a few seconds. Jaden thought she looked unsteady. Here she was threatening to somehow get rid of a six foot tall, aggressive bully. She stood up and took Ruth's arm. "Are you all right? Let me help you. Ruth, a nap would be good for you."

"Oh, it's just when I stand up I have to be really careful. Arthritis in the legs slows you down and my balance is certainly not what it used to be. A few seconds and I will be fine."

Jaden hugged her. "I'm going to talk to Bill as soon as I can. I will ask for complete secrecy before I say anything to the police. Maybe I should see a lawyer first."

Driving back to the store, Jaden's thoughts whirled around her like the colored glass scenes in a kaleidoscope. The relief she felt finding Laura alive was a big comfort. But how to keep her safe? They needed advice. By the time Jaden reached Sixth Street, she realized help happened to live next door. General Edward Stennis, Esther's son, who retired to Carmel. Ex-spy or agent or whoever he was. The General was on an eternal search for a home in the area. Even for millionaires the property was overpriced. During the year-long search he lived with his mother. Jaden learned that Esther herself did some type of spy work during the cold war. She still had remarkable powers of observation. People often would not care what they said in front of her because of her "old woman" persona.

Jaden opened the store. Customers came right behind her. She helped three before she had a break to call Esther.

"Why don't you come over here? Eddie is cooking his specialty, meat stew supreme."

Her son, probably in his mid-sixties, was still Eddie to her.

"Sounds nice, Esther. I'll be there about 6:30. Is that O.K?"

"Yes, dear. We haven't seen you in a while. It'll be nice to catch up."

That would be so pleasant if the subject were not deadly serious.

Her first goal was to keep Laura alive. Jeff was capable of murder. The drinking made him worse, hot tempered and violent. Jaden thought he might be just as bad sober because he liked to bully people. Those threatening emails showed some more mental problems. Frustration. He always took that out on Laura. Jaden knew he was a coward, too. That did not make him any less dangerous because cowards work in the dark. They must hide their true intentions, wrap them in plausible lies for the gullible to drop their guard. Daylight, the brilliant sun, on them would make them scurry for their dark coffins like vampires.

As he was an adult, Jaden knew Jeff's behavior probably would not change.

Normally she was always delighted to visit with Esther. With her son, Edward, they made the most interesting pair in the village. They were working on a fiction book that she knew would contain some of the actual events of their lives. They had both been spies. She could not wait to read it.

The distinguished, silver-haired retired general opened the door for her. He hugged her. She wondered how many hearts he had broken through the years. She could feel he was still muscular. He and Esther walked to the beach every day. He went to the sports center to work out, usually before lunch.

"Jaden!" Esther called from the kitchen, which was off the living room. The apartments had a bathroom opposite the kitchen and two bedrooms. There were six apartments. Since every apartment had the same floor plan, what was amazing was how different each one looked inside.

"What smells so good?"

"Meat stew supreme," Edward Stennis answered. "A specialty of the house."

"I call it garbage stew," Esther took off her apron. "Eddie thought it needed a slightly classier name. Can't say that hobo might be any classier. But meat stew supreme sounds elegant. We could translate it to French."

"When we were out on survival, we threw in anything we could find in a pot and ate it. Amazing what you will eat when you are hungry." The retired general grinned.

"This is a close second," Esther told her. "It often contains whatever I can find in the kitchen, vegetables that should not be sitting around any longer, leftover meat, potatoes, onions, broth made into gravy disguises it all."

"This smells delicious. Thank you for having me over."

"Would you like a glass of wine? Then you can tell us the problem. Sit down. You look a little flushed. Have you been sick?""

"Thanks, Edward. After I tell you the story you will understand why."

And she went through the whole novella. A few times she stopped to wipe away tears.

When she finally stopped, both Esther and Edward said nothing.

She finally took another sip of the smooth Monterey Riesling.

Edward sighed. "It isn't often that I'm speechless, Jaden. What a difficult situation."

"You haven't told Bill?" Esther asked. "You must as soon as possible."

"He's on the late shift tonight. I have to tell the police. Hoped I could offer a solution to keep Laura's location a secret."

"That is the most important thing." Edward took a carrot from the vegetable tray that Esther had made for snacks. "And it won't be easy. Jeff is a drunk and a bully, but from my experience he also is calculating and very dangerous."

"I know," Jaden answered in almost a whisper. "He's unpredictable."

"The thing for her to do is appear and then disappear," Esther suggested.

"A witness protection program," Edward suggested. "I know some people I could contact. The trouble is Laura will have to make an appearance to show that she is alive. That will put her in danger." He sat back and closed his eyes as if he were day dreaming. More likely he was going through all the possibilities of disappearing a person.

"Bobbi managed to fool us for several months when she moved here," Esther reminded them. "She turned out to be wonderful with disguises. Laura's appearance could be changed."

"There's several ways to do this, but Laura and the police have to decide on a course of action" Edward added. "In the meantime let me make some inquires. I know people who could help. The witness protection program is for specific situations. Laura may not qualify. But there are other ways to help her into a new life."

"My guess is that Laura would not mind disappearing. The store is probably bankrupt anyway. They weren't able to pay the next month's lease. She knows staying away from Jeff is critical. It took her a long time and a lot of hurt to figure that out." Jaden imagined they had helped others disappear before.

Esther took two hot pads from a drawer to lift the stew to the table. "I think the women are like brainwashed prisoners. They try to please the abuser. If they are lucky, they finally realize they need to get away or be permanently injured or killed."

Jaden offered, "Bobbi had a court order to keep her husband away. He ignored that and attacked her. You know how that ended. In a struggle in the kitchen, Bobbi's husband slipped and fell on the knife he was holding. But a District Attorney who wanted to make a name for herself charged her with first degree murder. She was accused of 'Luring him to the house.' And of stalling the 911 call until he bled to death.

The story dominated the media for three months. Luckily Bobbi Jones' attorney, MacKenzie Anderson, destroyed the case against her. She still needed to escape. Her friend, who managed the library in Carmel, offered her a job. Bobbi rented number three of the Dolores Court Apartments. It was two months before Jaden realized who she was.

"Dinner is served," Esther announced.

After Esther put the steaming stew pot on the table they sat down.

"The dressing on this spinach salad is delicious. The strawberries give it a tantalizing flavor." Jaden commented after her first bite.

"Mom makes her own dressings. This one is a rice vinegar and olive oil with fresh strawberries," Edward explained.

"She could give Sydney at the café downstairs some salad dressing lessons," It's delicious without being too sweet."

Edward promised her, "I'll have some answers for you tomorrow about how to help Laura disappear. Once her husband knows she is alive she won't be safe."

Jaden imagined they had helped people disappear before.

Back in her apartment, she did not sleep right away. Her mind whirled with everything that had happened. Finding Laura alive was a tremendous relief. Finding that she had finally decided to get away from her situation was the best news she could ever get. Now, how to keep her safe? Finally she fell into a deep, dreamless sleep, thinking, *I am not going to allow Jeff to find her, to have the chance to attack her again.*

In the morning she woke in a groggy fog. She forced herself to grope through the mist toward the coffee pot. After two muscular cups of coffee and toast with honey, she finally called Bill.

She woke him saying only that she needed to talk to him immediately. Since he lived in apartment five, he came right over wearing his slacks with a pajama top. She wanted to hug him but offered him a cup of coffee instead.

"Would you like some toast?"

Bill nodded. "Now that I am awake. I thought someone might be breaking in."

Jaden sighed, "First, I need to tell you that Laura is alive."

"What?" Bill's toast fell in mid-bite. Orange marmalade splattered on his plate.

She told him what she knew about Laura's whole story. "Bill, once this is known you may have to release Jeff. There has to be a way to keep Laura safe. I don't think he will ever leave her alone. I have photos on my camera of how she was badly beaten. It's hard to believe."

"Where is she?"

"Can you keep her location a secret?"

"For now. I'll have to do a report. I am really glad she is alive. I was thinking the worst. We've already found out that the blood in the apartment was not Jeff's."

"Promise me or I won't tell you."

"How about this? If you bring her to the station and take her back, I won't know so could not reveal her location. If she files a complaint, we can keep him confined for several more days. He will probably get bailed out. He already has a public defender."

Jaden took another huge swallow of coffee. "We will only have a few days if that happens. When Jeff gets out Laura would not be safe."

"I know. And our six person police force can't watch him all the time. No matter what it's a really bad situation. There has to be a solution." He gave her a quick hug. "We will figure it out. I promise you. I'll set up a meeting and then call you. We will want her to be seen by a physician, too, so please tell her that is absolutely necessary."

"All right. Thank you, Bill."

"You are welcome." He gave her another hug that made her relax. "Things will work out."

They have to.

She had almost forgotten someone would have to open the store. And she was the only "someone."

Luckily, the work opening took her mind away from the problem of helping Laura. Several customers came in to keep her more occupied. By eleven a.m. she had not even checked the computer for new orders.

Bill called to ask her to bring Laura into the station at two p.m. if possible.

"I'll call right now," Jaden told him. "She's not far away."

She had already put Ruth's number in her phone. Ruth answered right away.

"Jaden," Ruth asked, "She will be safe? That husband will kill her."

"I'm not going to tell them where she is. Your name will not be mentioned. I'd like to pick Laura up at 1:45 if it's all right with her. Would you like me to talk to her now?"

"I'll explain, Jaden. I'll only call you if there is a problem."

"I'm working on keeping Laura safe. She's been through enough. Whatever I can do for her I will do. Believe me."

"Jaden, thanks sincerely. I've been so worried, but it's true. There is safety in numbers. All of my relatives are gone. There was no one else to tell the police what happened." Ruth's voice wavered.

"I'll be over at one forty-five. You stay at the house because we don't want anyone to connect you and Laura. Tell her to use the side door."

"I understand. Goodbye, Jaden." When she hung up the phone, all the sound in the store and from the street stopped. She closed her eyes and shook her head. The sounds returned to normal. The quiet had been in her imagination. Probably born of nervousness combined with fear about Laura. There was a darkness that she could not shake. Like the shadow of the grim reaper looming over the entire room. Jaden always paid attention to her premonitions. Ignoring those warnings plus her overwhelming curiosity had steered her into trouble so many times that Bill warned her to ignore them.

Curiosity killed the cat.

She came close in Big Sur. Her curiosity almost killed her.

Bobbi told her, "Some people live in the past, some in the present. They don't see tomorrow. Jaden, I think you have the talent of seeing flashes of the future. It is a gift although sometimes you may not think so."

"The gift" was warning her. Jaden didn't know what to do except that she had promised Ruth. She would not leave Laura's side. Someone else she just realized they needed was a lawyer. She would find out if MacKenzie Anderson was in Carmel or in San Diego. He was a super attorney, not a cheap one, she knew, but one of the best. If anyone could help Laura it would be MacKenzie. The problem was the nature of abusers. They were often fixated for whatever reason. And extremely devious.

No way could she or anyone else stay with Laura every minute.

Jeff won't get near her when I'm around. Remembering Ruth's voice, she closed her eyes and prayed that Jeff would not be released.

Maybe they could lock him up and lose the key. Once they realized Laura was still alive he could not be held on suspicion of murder. Maybe she should have advised Laura to disappear with

General Stennis's help. But of course several people would know she was alive. It was Jeff's pure luck that the abused woman was not dead. She was covered with bruises and Jaden knew she had had at least one broken arm in the past. The thought made her stomach tighten. How could Laura stand it? It was some kind of miracle that Laura had survived this long. She thought back to that day that Ruth had brought in the orchid and a nervous Laura came in with suspicious injuries.

Jaden should have guessed at the time that Laura was near the breaking point.

When Jaden took Laura to the police station on Junipero, she tried not to stare. The woman's face was half black and blue. She slumped in the passenger seat with a moan as though she would like to disappear.

Bill let her sit in on the short interview as Laura explained how frightened she was.

"I...I decided to run away. He wasn't going to stop hitting me. Jeff was getting worse. He wasn't going to change...."

"Would you like some coffee or water?" Bill asked gently because Laura's eyes were filled with tears. She was in obvious pain.

Jaden handed her a tissue. Laura wiped her eyes. The gesture obviously hurt. She flinched and squeezed her eyes shut. Her eyes brimmed over with more tears.

Bill asked, "Sergeant Miller is going to take some pictures, Laura."

They stepped to the door to let the sergeant take the photos.

"Jaden, she has to go to the hospital," Bill whispered. "I'm going to make arrangements. It's really necessary. I'll let you know as soon as possible when she can be checked in."

"I understand, Bill."

Jaden explained the hospital stay to Laura on their short drive to Ruth's house.

She was so beaten down that she did not protest. Jaden walked her down the uneven slate path to Ruth's house. The older woman helped Laura in.

"Thank you," Ruth said quietly. Jaden waited until she heard the deadbolt click.

Jaden warmed a mug of milk to hopefully help her relax and sleep. A good night's sleep was what she prayed for tonight. The steaming milk worked after a few sips. Her eyelids felt heavy. Her elbow slipped off the side of the table. She juggled quickly to keep the cup from falling.

Go to bed. Bring the rest of the milk with you.

She slipped into her giant pajama tee shirt and slid under the covers. While she thought sleep would not come, after a few moments the blissful darkness swept her away from every worry. Birds singing in the morning always woke her. This time she woke to silence. First she always wiggled her toes to make sure they were working. Being in bed for so long recovering after being trapped in the caves in Big Sur left her muscles weak. She tried to walk and exercise. Recovery seemed to be slow and slower. Her salvation was Bill and all of her other friends in Carmel.

Jaden decided she needed to get up. She tried to push the covers away. Her arms would not move. Her toes were not moving. Her body was frozen. But her heart was drumming so loudly that she could hear it. A movement from the living room took the ghostly shape of a hovering, dark giant. Jaden tried to move as the form glided closer and closer. Next to her, it finally took shape.

Jeff was standing next to the bed.

His words came in echoing waves, "Hello, Jaden. You don't have your knife now." As the shadow loomed over her, she tried to scream. No sound came. She could not breathe. The shadow engulfed her like a creeping fog. Everything went black.

The paralyzing terror vanished to a peaceful morning. Jaden woke to a sparrow singing outside of her kitchen window. This time her toes did wiggle. Her hands were trembling. She slowly realized the terrifying nightmare was just that. She pushed the covers back and sat on the side of the bed. *She breathed deeply. This nightmare was conjured up by her overactive imagination twisting the events of the day.*

"Dreams can be prophetic," she muttered to herself. At least two other times her dreams were a warning. This one was, too, though she did not need a dream to tell her that Jeff was dangerous.

"Strong coffee is what I need." Jaden stood up. She did not care how many warnings about coffee there were floating around the universe. Before she headed for the coffee pot, she checked for her Monarch knife in the pocket of her jacket that she had thrown over a dining chair.

The knife was like an old friend. Her late husband, Brent, had it specially made for her.

She put two pieces of wheat bread in the toaster. It was hardly a fancy breakfast. With butter and honey it would do until lunch-time at the Mad Hatters.

The first hour at the shop dragged because she was waiting for Bill's message. The phone rang. A customer. Normally, she would be glad because it usually meant a sale. This time she was distracted waiting for the message she really wanted from Bill.

Finally, he called on her cell phone, which she snatched to answer immediately.

"Jaden, can you bring Laura to the hospital tomorrow morning? We want her to be examined by a doctor. I asked if there was a private room. Everything is arranged with a physician who does many of these abuse cases.

"Bill, that is great. Jeff won't be out yet?" A deep sigh of relief helped her to relax. *This would work out.*

Bill popped her temporary bubble of relaxation by saying, "Jaden, once we are positive Laura is alive we can't keep Jeff in jail much longer. He would be guilty of assault but not murder. And Laura has to sign the complaint. Even so, he might get out way too soon."

"After all this that she certainly would sign a complaint about him."

"You would be surprised. Sometimes for some ungodly reason they change their minds. They think the guy will be different."

"This time I don't think so. It's because she left her purse."

"Her purse?"

"It's a girl thing. Women and their purses are a team. She left without her purse. No money. No car keys. That means she wanted to escape."

"Let's pray it's not as bad as that sounds. Sorry about all of this."

Jaden hesitated, "I love you." It was the first time she had actually said it aloud. The thought had been there for months. She wondered if Bill realized what she had said.

Life would be empty without him. He was the opposite of Brent. He was good natured and relaxed most of the time. For so long she felt that finding someone else was like being disloyal to her dead husband. He had been her best friend. After five years, she was upset to realize that she sometimes had to look at his picture to recall his face.

She wondered if Bill realized what she had said. He didn't say anything in response.

Her next call was to the attorney's Carmel office.

"Jaden. It's good to hear from you," MacKenzie Anderson answered.

"You may not think so after you hear the problem. Are you in Carmel?"

"Just so happens that I am. I come up here when I want to get away from it all. This condo is so peaceful. I come here any time I can. What is the problem? I'm not at the office so take your time."

She went through the whole story, editing when she could. At the end she heard him sigh. He cleared his throat.

"And I thought I had heard it all."

"I know. Bobbi and I did our best to help. Somehow I ended up deeply involved. I would do anything to help Ruth. There has to be a way to help Laura. I know she needs an attorney's advice. Laura and Jeff were close to losing the failing business."

"Let's see if I can do anything to help first. It's very important that I meet and interview Laura as soon as possible."

"What are you doing this afternoon?"

After telling him about the hospital, she called Ruth on her cell phone.

"Jaden, it's going to take a lot to encourage Laura to leave the house, even to a hospital. I'm very worried about her mental state. It's not surprising considering what happened to her."

"I know, Ruth. At least she finally decided to leave her husband. It was a huge decision. I'll come over at 1:30. You stay home because we don't want anyone to see you two together."

"I understand. Jaden. It's impossible to thank you for what you have done."

The next one to call was Hal Lamont to see if he could work for her this afternoon. She hoped he was home because there was no one else who could run the store without training.

Hal sold her the cutlery store, A Slice of Carmel. He was also their landlord. When she bought the business; he asked her if she would like to manage the six upstairs apartments. She would get hers for free in exchange. The best bargain in the world considering the rents in the area. Hal worked with her for the first year. After that he often substituted or helped her when the shop was too busy. For two months while she was recuperating from exposure and dehydration, Hal ran the shop. Jaden considered him part angel.

"Sure, Jaden. I can help this afternoon. Not tomorrow because Sandy and I are having company. Her sist and brother-in-law."

"I may not be back today before five. Is that all right?"

"No problem. Are you feeling OK? We worry about your health."

"I'm fine. I'll tell you all about it one of these days. Right now I can't."

"Jaden, I'll be over as soon as I can."

"Thanks so much, Hal."

At noon she closed the shop to have lunch at The Mad Hatter's. She had tried everything on the menu. Jaden loved every dish, every sandwich, every salad Sydney made. Luckily she seemed to be able to eat a lot because she had lost fifteen pounds while she was recovering. That bit of fortune would not last forever. She already put back five of them. If she was not careful, some day she might wake up seeing a snowman shape in her mirror.

Kyle came over to the table right away with a steaming mug of one of her favorites, raspberry tea.

"Jaden, dear, you do need to get out more. This should perk you up." He sat down next to her. "Is there something you want to confess? Is it Bill? That would not surprise me. He's moody sometimes. Is he trying to take advantage of you? He isn't the type to understand 'no'."

"You are a shameless gossip."

"I know. What else is there to do around here when I am not helping customers?"

"Bill is a wonderful man." She squeezed lemon into the tea. Jaden fought the temptation to tell Kyle that she loved Bill. It would be all over Carmel by tomorrow. Kyle already realized or he would not have mentioned him.

"Uh, ha. I agree." He stood up.

"It's something I can't talk about right now."

"O.K. What would you like today?"

"How about a bowl of Sydney's clam chowder?" With the way her stomach had been churning all morning, the chowder ought to be perfect. Sydney's was the best in the village.

"You've got it." On the way back to the kitchen he dropped menus off at another table. The café was filling up fast as it always did at noontime.

Kyle returned almost immediately with the chowder. She knew he made one of those giant pots of creamy clam chowder every day. One of the rare times there was some left at the end of their day, 4 p.m., Kyle would offer it to her saying that they would have to throw it away.

"Enjoy" he told her, "And, Jaden, relax. We worry about you."

"Thanks, Kyle. I know how much I can count on you and Sydney."

"Jaden, any time."

He smiled broadly and moved to take orders from the tourists at the next table.

The warm soup and tea, the bright sun, all combined to calm her. She took a deep breath. If only she could just stay here for the rest of the afternoon. She thought about how lucky she was to have friends like Hal and Kyle and Bobbi. Jaden made herself stand up. She picked up her purse and headed for the stairs down to the parking garage underneath the court.

The underground lot always made her nervous. Sergio Manetti was murdered with a knife from her store. First the police blamed her and then Bobbi Jones. That's when Bobbi called her lawyer, MacKenzie Anderson. That's also when they found out who Bobbi really was, the notorious Roberta Petra-Jones. MacKenzie's practice was in San Diego, but he liked Carmel so much that he bought a condo here.

Jaden turned the car onto Carpenter St. Ten minutes later she was pulling up in front of Ruth's Seabreeze house.

Ruth let her in, saying, "Laura is really nervous but she understands why the requests to go to the hospital and see the attorney. Jaden, I can't thank you enough for what you have been doing for her. She has to get free of that husband or he will kill her. I know it."

Jaden swallowed hard. She felt the same way. All she could do was nod.

They went to Laura's room. She was sitting on the side of the bed with a frightened deer look on her face. Ruth sat down next to her and hugged her. "Everything will be all right. Laura, You have friends like Jaden who will help you."

Laura looked up at Jaden with clear blue eyes rimmed red with crying. Jaden could barely look at the bruised left side of Laura's face. How often had he hit her? She actually must be pretty strong to have survived this long.

"Ruth told you we were going to the hospital? It's very close."

Laura looked down at the floor, nodding. She swallowed hard and stood up.

To the abused woman this must seem like the last mile. I'll be really happy for a doctor to check her. She needed a doctor's care.

She took Laura's arm and led her through the front door to the car. Ruth closed the door. Jaden heard the dead bolt click. She felt thankful that the distance to the hospital, CHOMP, was short.

"Jaden," Laura finally spoke, "Thank you for what you said about my having friends. Jeff never liked me to have friends over. He had something bad to say about everyone. Nobody was ever good enough. My parents are gone. I felt like I was all alone in the world. Ruth has been so wonderful. She said Jeff would never touch me again."

Out of the corner of her eye Jaden saw that Laura was wiping the tears with trembling fingers. *Her mental state is really bad. She probably needs to be in treatment of some sort. Can't get her to the hospital soon enough.*

Jaden exited at Highway 68. Fortunately the hospital was next to the highway on the Monterey side. She spotted the Carmel Police car parked next to it.

Bill emerged from the car. She was so glad to see her policeman that she had to fight back the urge to hug him.

"I wanted to walk you into the hospital," he told her, walking around to the passenger side to open the door. "Laura, everything will be all right. Jaden and I will stay with you."

Laura came out slowly. Bill held her arm gently as they walked together toward the front glass doors of the hospital. Their reflections showed in the glass as the automatic doors opened. Inside the large lobby, MacKenzie was waiting for them. He shook hands with Bill.

"MacKenzie, this is Laura," Jaden introduced them. She noticed MacKenzie's somber expression.

By this time Laura was trembling. If he saw that or her obvious injuries, he kept silent. His mouth was set in a grim straight line. Jaden guessed he was struggling to keep his temper. To be honest, she felt the same way.

Bill came over to them with a Doctor Edwards. He shook hands with MacKenzie and introduced them to Doctor Kay Hamilton who immediately went to Laura. It was obvious who needed an exam.

"Laura," Dr. Hamilton asked, "would you come with me? Bill, you know where the cafeteria is if you would like to have coffee. We will be a while with the examination."

Laura gave Jaden a pleading glance and turned to go with the doctor. Her head was down and her shoulders slumped.

Jaden wanted to follow and stay with her the whole time. She knew better. She was not Laura's mother or sister so could not insist.

Bill spoke up, "I know what you're thinking, Jaden. Laura is going to have to face things on her own. Dr. Hamilton is great. Sadly, she's seen women in worse condition than Laura's."

"I just don't understand why they stay and take that punishment." Jaden repeated her thought for probably the tenth time.

"And they are isolated," Jaden offered. "Laura was telling me in the car that Jeff deliberately isolated her. Her parents were gone. It was only by accident that she knew where Ruth lived. The women can't get any advice or help from any friends."

"Only when the abuse gets so bad that they can't stand it anymore do they take any action. Usually they want to protect their children, but it's way too late," Bill added.

Jaden realized what he meant. They entered the swinging doors to the cafeteria.

Bill asked, "Who would like coffee? Be prepared to drink several cups."

They found a booth in the corner, which was about as private as possible. Bill brought them three steaming mugs from a giant urn. "MacKenzie, do you need sugar or cream?"

"I take it black, thanks."

They were three black coffee kindred spirits, which helped a lot. Mackenzie's first question was, "How is Bobbi doing?"

"I think we are going to hear an announcement about her marrying David Bartlett very soon. She is debating with herself because she will be living in such a remote spot. But considering her life after her husband died, in many ways she really likes the idea of getting away from it all. I can't blame her." Jaden took a deep sip of the strong coffee.

"I can understand that, too. It seems like I'm not doing well with the women in Carmel. I've known Bobbi for four years and Bartlett met her when? Six months ago? My ego is suffering. But if anyone deserves a good rest of her life, it's Roberta Petra Jones."

Jaden explained how Bobbi tried to help Laura. "It didn't seem to help."

MacKenzie looked thoughtful and finally said, "You can give people advice for a hundred years but unless they realize it *themselves*, and want to take action *themselves*, nothing will ever change. They rationalize and accept blame for everything. Bobbi was finally able to take charge of her own life as much as she could. Most of her world was stolen by media vultures. I often wonder if there are any real newspaper reporters anymore. They printed every ugly rumor and even made up stories. I was able to get a civil judgment for her from one dishonest paper. Too late. The damage to her reputation was already done."

"I hope you can help Laura."

He grinned. When MacKenzie smiled, his sky blue eyes twinkled. Of course, he must realize that Bill was obviously doing more than cooking when it came to their relationship. Jaden knew that behind his façade was a quick, brilliant mind. The lawyer's boyish looks fooled many, including other attorneys and media people.

She felt extremely grateful that he was willing to help Laura.

"I know you've had a long recovery, Jaden. You are going to be completely well. It may take a while, but it will happen."

The frown on Bill's forehead deepened. He and all of her friends repeatedly told her the same thing. Their positive thoughts pulled her through the toughest part of recovery. Some days she felt so weak that she wanted to give up and never get out of bed. Finally she forced herself to walk a few steps at a time. Most of those times Bill was right there to support her, make her walk.

Her indefensible, thoughtless journey into the caves under the Bartlett house in Big Sur almost killed her. She could not explain to anyone that she was compelled to the deadly journey by a force that she could not fight against.

Bill was right to be angry. She almost died for a stupid mistake. Trouble was it was not her first stupid mistake. She looked at Bill, who was staring at her with those dark, flashing eyes. He knew about her mistakes and he still loved her.

"I'm doing well, MacKenzie. My friends here have been my reason for recovering. Bill even cooked meals for me."

"Can you fill me in on exactly the information about Laura that you have?" MacKenzie asked. "I'll ask Laura for her view of the story. I assume she is the only eye witness."

"That's right," Bill took a long sip of his coffee. "Jeff was drunk and says he does not remember anything except the table was set for dinner. He woke up. There was blood in the room and Laura was gone. There was blood on the bed, the floor, and the small kitchen table. The lab report stated that the blood was not Jeff's. We all thought he had killed her and disposed of the body. I thought he was lying about not remembering. The trouble is we have seen this situation way too much. He is a severe alcoholic. Drinks from seven a.m. on. The bills show that he is buying a fifth of vodka almost every day. He's been a mess in custody. The doctor we use suggested he go right into rehab. If he keeps drinking, he will kill himself. He will fall or bleed to death."

MacKenzie shook his head. "Jaden, how did you get involved?"

She explained how Laura came into the shop when Ruth was delivering orchids. They both realized right away that something was wrong. "I think she had a broken arm not six months earlier. She told us then that she fell off the front steps. This time she hit the side of her face and broke her glasses. She claimed it was another fall. Laura was not a clumsy person. Besides she was acting like a whipped puppy. Ruth and I both sensed what was going on. Why didn't she tell someone about the abuse?'"

"And this is why she went to Ruth," MacKenzie guessed. "Jeff made sure she had no friends to help her. She did not figure on you or Bobbi or Ruth."

"Jaden doesn't miss much," Bill told him, "but sometimes she lets her curiosity take over. It usually makes trouble. And for sure can be dangerous." He managed to glare at her.

She knew he was right.

Jaden could not remember how many times her Carmel police sergeant had warned her about her curiosity. She knew very well that going into the smuggler's caves under the Bartlett House almost killed her. Bill could not stop reminding her. He told her it was because he loved her. He did not want to lose her. At this point Jaden knew she loved him, too. She could not imagine life without him. Every time he left the apartment she wanted him to stay.

MacKenzie asked, "Was Laura's blood identified at the scene?"

"According to her driver's license it was the same type. There was no way to quickly identify the blood as hers, but I don't think there's any doubt that she was bleeding heavily that night. There were two bloody towels in the bathroom. She probably took another towel when she left. It makes me so angry that these guys are such cowardly bullies. Jaden called his bluff when he came into the store threatening her about Laura's disappearance. Was he surprised! I asked another officer to arrest him. Afraid I would lose my temper."

Bill's frown deepened. She knew he hated these abuse cases anyway. Even though she only knew about

Bobbi Petra Jones and Laura, Jaden could not blame him for what he must have seen in his work.

Bill did have a temper that he usually kept well under control. Her husband, Brent, was even tempered. Their personalities were almost opposite.

MacKenzie looked from Bill to her with a quick smile on his face. She smiled, too. Bill's lips set in a straight line..

"Would you like more coffee?" Bill's chair scraped the floor as he stood up.

"Much as I like coffee," Jaden stared into her half-filled cup, "three cups is my limit. With this hospital visit and the caffeine I may never go to sleep tonight."

Bill grinned. Jaden knew what he was thinking. If he came over, she would sleep like a happy baby. When he was not there, the apartment felt empty.

MacKenzie joined Bill at the coffee urn. This time he took half a cup and added a half a cup of milk. "I have the feeling this is going to be a long day. I'm like Jaden, though. After lunch the caffeine will keep me from sleep.

Bill's cell phone rang. He took one look but didn't answer. He looked up to say, "The doc would like to see us now. Bring your coffee. It's OK."

"I hope you can help Laura, MacKenzie. Her husband had her beaten and brainwashed for eight years. She had that prisoner mentality. Bobbi understood how Laura's life became a nightmare that destroyed her mentally and physically."

Bill popped her temporary bubble of relaxation by saying, "Jaden, once we say Laura is alive we can't keep Jeff in jail much longer. He would be guilty of assault but not murder. And Laura has to sign the complaint. Will she do that? Even so he might get out."

"I would think after all this that she would sign a complaint."

"Sometimes, for some ungodly reason, they change their minds. They think the guy will be different. Somehow they feel it's their fault."

"This time I don't think so. Laura was so desperate she left with nothing. No wallet. No credit card. She wanted to get away from her whole life."

Bill responded to the message,. "Yes. We will be right over to Laura's room. 230? Thank you so much, doctor."

The trio put their coffee mugs on a tray by the door to the corridor.

"Room 230," Bill repeated. "The last room at the end of the hall. The doctor will meet us in front of the door."

The highly polished white floor in the hall gleamed so brightly that it hurt Jaden's eyes to look down. Dr. Hamilton met them, a deep frown creasing her forehead. "Laura is getting dressed. I wanted her to stay overnight because of her injuries, but she refused. She's frightened that her husband will find her. I understand. She has old injuries, too. Years of abuse." She shook her head. "By tomorrow you will have my complete report. I've given her medication for relaxation. I'll prescribe it for two weeks. If it helps her we will renew. It's not a permanent solution. The medication is strong. Laura could benefit from seeing a psychiatrist. Right now she's not open to that. She's still in shock."

Jaden suggested, "Later, when she feels safe. I'm not sure when that would be possible."

The doctor asked, "Bill, How long can you keep the husband in jail?"

"Not much longer," Bill answered, "Once it is known that Laura is alive it is no longer a murder charge. The new charge will be assault. The public defender will get him out. We can't watch him all the time."

Jaden felt her own stomach knot. She already knew what Jeff was like. *Dangerous.*

"Doctor," MacKenzie asked, "When do you think that I could speak to Laura alone? I am her attorney. I need to have her version of the events."

The doctor told them, "Laura is worried that her husband will find her. I understand. To answer your question I'll go in with you," she answered, "and if she seems calm enough then I will leave you with her. She's been through a nightmare ordeal for several years. The duty nurse will be right there. If Laura starts to get upset, stop right away."

"I'll wait or come in with you," Jaden offered. "She knows me."

"That's a good idea," the doctor agreed. "It might keep her calm. I would like to keep her here at least two more hours. Several days would be better so she could have a complete rest."

"I'm going to call my captain." Bill took out his cell phone. "There's a waiting area by the nurses' station."

Laura looked as white as the sheets of the hospital bed. She managed a weak, thin smile on swollen lips.

Jaden began, "This is MacKenzie Anderson. One of the best attorneys in California. Laura."

The battered face managed a weak smile. "I've heard of you even before Jaden told me. Thank you for coming here."

MacKenzie put his hand on Laura's.

She flinched.

The reaction reminded Jaden of a terrified stray puppy that she had found once. They took in the abandoned terrier mix, who, with love, gradually became a happy addition to the family. *Brownie.* She hoped that would happen to Laura. Jaden's chest tightened. She could hear her own heart pounding. For a few seconds she saw nothing but a gray mist. She blinked.

She had a lot of faith in the lawyer.

"Laura," MacKenzie touched her hand. She flinched again but did not yank her hand away. "Could you tell me what happened the day and night you went to Ruth's? Take your time. We are here to listen to you."

Laura nodded and began her story. At first she choked and could not speak. Tears welled up in her red rimmed eyes.

MacKenzie pulled a tissue from the bedside tray. Laura dabbed her eyes and then blew her nose.

"It's all right," he said. "Would you like some ice water?"

She nodded. Jaden handed her the plastic cup with a straw.

White faced Laura sipped the water. Jaden would have given anything for the woman's complexion to return to a flesh tone. *I wonder if she is ever going to recover from the trauma.*

"I understand how hard this is for you." MacKenzie's voice was soft and soothing. Just the tone made Jaden relax. She saw that the same thing was happening to Laura.

She squeezed her eyes shut and prayed that Laura would get well enough to lead a normal life. That would be difficult at best.

Laura told the whole grizzly story. "I heard him unlock the front door of the shop and shuffle up the stairs. I knew he had been drinking. He drinks all day. Heard him bump from one side of the stairs to the other. I started toward the fridge to get out a tv dinner.

'Where's dinner?' he yelled.

'Be ready in a minute, Jeff.'

I warmed the tv dinner and put it on the table, then turned to get the bread and butter. He grabbed my shoulder

'Can't you cook real food?'

'I didn't know when you were coming home. It's good, Jeff. I had one.'

He shook me and I dropped the bread and the butter dish. It broke.

'You made me do that!' He was twisting my arm so that I cried,

'Please, Jeff, That hurts!'

'You baby,' He punched my arm. 'That's what hurts.' He hit my arm again. I grabbed it and could not stop the tears.

'I'll teach you to cook a decent meal!' I tried to duck but he hit my ear. Then my nose. I could feel the oozing of warm blood. He hit me again. Everything went black.

When I woke up on the floor blood was pouring from my nose. The front of my sweater was soaked. I grabbed a kitchen towel from the rack under the sink. When I pressed on my nose it stung so badly that my eyes filled with tears.

Jeff was in a chair, snoring. I looked at him and what I was saw a mean, bullying drunk. *I have to get out of here before he wakes up.* Every part of me throbbed. Each movement was like hundreds of needles were stabbing me at once. *I have to get away.* I crawled to the bathroom and pulled a bath towel from the rack. Jeff snorted. *Please, please, don't wake up.* When the water stung like bee stings on my arms I quit. Wrapped the towel around my neck and crawled to the top of the stairs. Scooted down them on my tail. Pulled myself up on the post at the bottom of the stair railing. The display cabinets braced me while I inched toward the front door. Took all my strength to open the door and stumble out on the sidewalk." She gasped in air.

MacKenzie was taking notes. "Go on."

The woman looked at them through half shut, red rimmed eyes. Her right eye was black and swollen. "There were people on the sidewalk, in the restaurants, all talking and having a good time. No one noticed me because it was getting dark and misty... Crossed Carpenter Street without even looking out for cars."

Laura sounded like she had a bad cold. "I decided to never go back. The pain was so bad. Why hadn't I taken a bottle of aspirin but did not know if that would have killed me or just made me sick. I was shuffling down Carpenter Street like a zombie. Everything was blurry. One time I collapsed under a bush and fell asleep for about half an hour. When I woke up my body was trembling. I dragged myself up and could not stop crying. My tears were salty mixed with the sweet taste of blood. The taste made my stomach cramp. The only thing I missed was *I should have my driver's license.* My purse was in the loft. The credit cards were maxed out. I was never going back there, license or not.

Could not reason what to do. If I threw myself into the highway traffic who would miss me? Took a deep breath that hurt like my ribs were broken. Maybe they were.

From then on only took shallow breaths that made walking difficult.

Then I remembered that Ruth lived up the hill. Her street was at the edge of Carmel. The next street over was the city of Monterey. I saw the metal pillars through a watery haze. *Ruth lives up there.* Felt sure she would help me. That hope carried me up the hill to Seabeeze Court. She lived on the cul-de-sac at the end. Stumbled again. My whole body was trembling until I passed out." Tears welled up in her eyes.

MacKenzie handed her another tissue.

Jaden reached out to grasp Laura's trembling hand. "It's all right. We're here and you will be safe now. Do you feel like telling us anymore?"

Laura nodded. "There's not much more. Forced myself down the slate path to the door and leaned against the doorbell. Ruth looked through the viewer before she opened it. She put her arms around me and helped me into the house. Ruth wanted me to go to the hospital. I was too afraid."

Jaden could hear her own heart drumming. How much longer would Laura have lived if she stayed with Jeff? Would she be strong enough to stay on her own? Probably not. Right now she was with Ruth. What was going to happen to her? Jaden felt so tired herself that she was tempted to look for an empty hospital room and sleep for twenty-four hours at least.

Somehow she managed to dredge up enough energy to wait until Laura was discharged and take her home. It took another hour for Laura to be released. This was against the doctor's recommendation and Jaden's better judgment

Right after the interview with Laura, Bill told them, "My captain wants an in person report. I'll be at the station. Jaden, I'll call you tonight."

MacKenzie stayed with Jaden and helped Laura into the car when they left the hospital. In the parking lot he told her,

"Jaden, I'll be working on this and have a staff member in my San Diego office research the law and cases like Laura's. The sad thing is there are way too many."

"MacKenzie, you are an angel."

"Would you like me to help, come to Ruth's with you?"

"That's not necessary" she told him, "Thank you for everything."

Jaden drove Laura back to Ruth's home. The closer they got to Seabreeze Court the more relaxed

Laura became. They walked together to the front door. Ruth answered the doorbell. She took Laura's hand. "Come in. I've been worried."

"Can I help?" Jaden asked.

"I'm all right. Jaden, thank you," Laura almost smiled. Not quite.

Jaden was so tired that she did not insist on helping. "Here is her medication. Ruth, the instructions are on the containers. Call me if you need anything." She made certain that Laura was in bed before she went out the front door. Only after she heard the sound of the deadbolt Jaden returned to her car.

Jaden did not hear from MacKenzie or Laura for over two weeks. A small voice in the back of her mind whispered that calling Ruth would be a good idea. She was busy with the store, making sales, filling online orders. Much as she prayed that Laura's situation would correct itself, the uneasiness never completely vanished from her thoughts. No news is good news. Laura must be doing well. She felt certain they would not call anyone except for Jaden or MacKenzie with new information. She knew the lawyer would be on top of everything.

Three more peaceful weeks went by. Jaden worried about Laura when she thought about her. She called every week but only spoke to Ruth. "Laura is doing well." Same answer every time.

The work at the store kept her busy enough to put Laura's sad experience at the back of her mind.

One Tuesday afternoon the shop phone rang about two p.m.

"Jaden?" She heard the obvious tremor in Ruth's voice. "Could you...could you come over to my house?"

Something was wrong. Jaden gasped in a short breath. *Laura.* Something had happened to Laura. She knew it was a mistake to let her go back to Ruth's. The doctor had told them that she would advise Laura to stay in the hospital for observation at least two nights. Then to a nursing home.

It had crossed Jaden's mind that a suicide watch might be necessary. That was entirely possible after everything that had happened to the battered woman.

"I'll come as soon as I can, Ruth."

"Thanks so much."

Jaden's hands shook as she set down the phone. There was no way she could keep the store open now. She called Hal. There was no answer so she left a message. She walked over to the door of the shop and turned the sign to *Closed*. Her fingers were still trembling.

The sense of doom that she recognized from past tragic times washed over her. For a few seconds she was afraid she would drown in the nightmare sensation. It was like the terror when she was trapped in the caves under the Bartlett house in Big Sur. Her escape from the rising ocean tide was incredible luck or a miracle. Over time she felt certain that the ghosts of the haunted point led her out of the cavern to tell others the answer to the mysterious disappearance of Rosalba Bartlett. That was the only explanation for surviving.. Finding her way to the opening to the Bartlett graveyard was a miracle. Everyone said so. Only Jaden felt that supernatural forces good and bad were behind the nightmare and her salvation.

Jaden took her purse out of the desk, pulled out her keys. Once outside she caught Kyle's eye as he was walking back to the café kitchen. "Kyle, I have to leave the shop right way. It's closed. Hal might come over if he gets my message. Would you mind telling anyone who asks that we will be open as soon as possible?

"Of course. What is the matter? Need help?"

"Kyle, thanks. I will call you if you can do anything." She turned to go toward the steps down to the parking garage.

"Sydney and I are always here for you, Jaden. Call us any time."

"I will," she said as she headed down the six concrete steps to the parking garage. Heart pounding, she pressed unlock on her key as she neared the car. Jaden always felt nervous in the garage. She often kept her hand on her Monarch knife in her pocket. This morning she even forgot to do that.

Be careful. In your state you could easily hit one of the posts or another car. The small garage had eight parking spaces-hers, Kyle, Sydney, Bobbi, Esther, (her son, General Stennis, used the space.) There were two unused spaces. *Three, really.* There was a space for the ghost tenant, Emile Von Otto. Von Otto rarely visited and when he did he drove a different car each time. Jaden was totally mystified by the eclectic makes. Some left oil spots. Some did not. Something nagged at her about the different cars and the fact that although she was the apartment manager she had never seen Von Otto. She was curious enough to do an internet search for his name, which yielded 0 results. Every so often he left a sack of trash in the garage cans. Someday those dots would connect. She would finally meet the most elusive man in the world. Now she needed to get over to Ruth's.

By the time she reached Carpenter Street, Jaden's heart had actually slowed to a normal beat. Ruth sounded so upset. Laura must be too much for the older woman to handle. She turned left onto highway one, and almost immediately exited at Del Monte Boulevard. Then left at Donner.

She drove past the No Outlet sign at Seabreeze to the cul-de-sac. Pulling into Ruth's driveway was as close as she could get to the front door. Her heart started racing again. By this time she realized her nerves were not as good as she had hoped. Jaden watched her forefinger tremble as she rang the bell.

No answer.

She pressed the bell again.

Someone was walking to the front double doors. The small window in the door opened. She was surprised and relieved to see Laura staring at her with huge eyes that seemed to take up a third of her pale face.

"Hello, Jaden. Come in." Her brief smile came and went quickly. Laura looked...Laura looked... Jaden tried to think. She was...different. Her face looked normal again, thank God. At least she was alive. Jaden had been imagining all sorts of frightening possibilities. Here she was, standing calmly in the front hall.

"Ruth called me. She sounded so upset that I came right over. Laura, what's happened? Is Ruth all right?"

"She's not feeling well. She wants to talk with you. Come with me." Laura sounded a little detached, but calm.

They walked down the hall to the back of the house. In her room the windows were fitted with shelves that held a number of orchids, some blooming, some not. The orchid lady was lying in her bed. She smiled weakly. Jaden reached out to her hand, which felt cold and limp. "Ruth, do you need to go to the doctor?"

Ruth's cold, blue veined hand tightened on hers. "Thank you for coming, Jaden. I didn't know what else to do. I've been to the doctor. Several doctors. Tests. I'm not going to get better. Did

Laura say anything to you?" She kicked her legs under the quilt on the bed.

"No." Jaden looked back to see that Laura was no longer in the hall.

"Good. She's been through enough. Jaden." She drew in a wheezy breath.

"I killed him."

Jaden thought she heard wrong. "Killed him?" she whispered. "Killed who?" Right now Ruth did not even look as though she could walk. How could she have killed someone? Did she want to confess something from years back? Laura had not seemed the least bit shocked or hysterical. If someone had died, Laura, of all people, would have fallen apart. Instead she looked strangely ultra-normal.

"He fell downstairs."

"Who fell downstairs?"

"Laura's husband, Jeffrey. He's there now. Downstairs. That's why I called you."

Jaden's mouth opened but the words came out in a choking whisper, "Here? Do you know he's dead? How did he find out where Laura was?"

"I don't know. Both Laura and I heard glass break. Laura ran out into the hall to see what happened. He was in the house and attacked Laura at the top of the stairs. I heard her screaming. I grabbed a knife from the kitchen and yelled "Get away from her!"

"He laughed at me. No, old lady! She's getting what she deserves!"

"I didn't say it, but thought, 'So are you.' He was choking her so I stabbed him in the side of his ribs. He fell down the stairs. *Two flights*. The fall might have killed him. Jaden, I did the stabbing. It was one of my sharpest knives so the blade went right in. I used all my strength, though. Laura had to catch me as my knees buckled. My hands shook. She helped me back here."

Laura joined them. "I was going to call 911," she said. "But there was no sound. I peered over the stair rail and saw him lying there. He wasn't moving. I came back to ask Ruth what to do. I still thought we should call 911. She said to wait until she felt strong enough to go downstairs. After an hour he had not moved. Finally Ruth felt well enough to go downstairs with me. We both took knives. He was dead." She was speaking like a monotone robot.

She said *he was dead* without any emotion at all. Jaden felt that uneasy sensation whirling around her. She had to force herself to stay still until the frightening whirling stopped.

He was dead echoed in her ears. Jaden had feared for Laura. Now Jeff was dead? She had to admit relief herself.

No sorrow.

"Ruth said, 'Everything would be fine. 'I know what to do. No one will know.' But she started to shake. She said she would have to go back to bed. We could take care of things later. Later she was not any better. That's why she called you. We could not finish her plan, whatever that was."

What plan could Ruth possibly have? Jaden forced out, "I'll have to call Bill." She cleared her throat. "And MacKenzie."

That nagging suspicions that often overwhelmed her common sense should go away. The feeling grabbed her as though it had arms, powerful arms. She swallowed hard and took several deep breaths. Semi-calmness returned. Her voice came out in another squeaky whisper. "I should see for myself." It was the last thing Jaden wanted to do..

"Go ahead, dear," Ruth tried to raise herself higher than the pillows. She struggled to get a little closer to Jaden. "He won't hurt anyone anymore." A half smile crossed her lips. She clutched the quilt with her veined hands and sank back down to the pillows. Ruth caught him when he was distracted. She did own the sharpest knives in Carmel. He easily could have lost his balance and fallen down the stairs after being stabbed. Jaden hoped Jeff died in the fall downstairs.

That story was plausible. An accidental death when the women were defending themselves.

Ruth suddenly clutched at her arm, pulling her right against the bed. "I'm not sorry, she whispered, "He was a mean, violent person. Laura is better off without him. You see what he did to her. The law would not hold him forever. She was always in danger. Laura may never recover from what that man did. At least he won't bother her anymore."

"I understand, Ruth. First I'll go downstairs to see Jeff. Then I will have to call Bill and MacKenzie. Police will be coming to the house. Do you realize that?"

"Yes." Ruth closed her eyes. For a few moments Jaden thought the woman had suddenly fallen asleep.

"Everything will be taken care of. Try not to worry. She was talking to herself as much as Ruth.

Eyes still closed, Ruth, in such a low voice that Jaden barely heard. "I'm not worried. Not at all. Now Laura is safe. He can't hurt her any more."

Her words made shivers travel up Jaden's arms as she quietly left the room.

Laura was standing outside in the hall. Her eyes seemed to take up at least a third of her face.

"Laura, I have to call the police and I'll call MacKenzie Anderson. You should speak to him before anyone else."

The woman's only response was to stare at a point beyond Jaden's shoulder into the open door of Ruth's room. If she was upset by her husband's death, Laura was burying reality far deeper than she should. After all the woman had been through, Jaden knew she had more problems than most people. The obvious, eerie detachment was understandable considering the situation..

Laura whispered, "She only has six months. Did you know she was so sick?"

Jaden gulped. *Oh, no.* Bright lights flashed in front of her eyes. Such a nice, sweet lady. *Not fair. Not fair.* She blinked. Her vision cleared. This was about as much bad news as she could stomach. The memory of Brent's death washed over her like an ocean wave. The shocking memory that she thought was buried forced her to struggle to control her shaking hands.

Jaden finally managed to say, "Laura, do you want to come downstairs with me?"

"Why?" Laura asked.

Maybe she had blocked out the whole incident. Jaden answered, "Because Jeff is downstairs. Do you know that Jeff is there and that he is dead?"

"Yes. And he will stay down there. Ruth said that when she was thinking clearly. He will never hurt me again." The last words came quietly but ominously. Jaden's arms felt shivery cold.

"I'm going downstairs. Will you watch Ruth? I think she's asleep right now."

"I'll watch her."

Jaden peered down the landing. She could not see anything except splotches of drying blood that must have sprayed helter skelter as the body fell. She started down the stairs carefully, avoiding the blood that certainly would be evidence. Everything started to whirl around her as though she were on an out of control carousel. Her hand slipped into her pocket to feel the Monarch that was her old friend. The world finally stopped whirling. Breathing deeply, she steadied herself against the rail. She did not need protection from a dead body.

Jaden spotted a hand, the five fingers spread out on the dark laminate flooring. The hand seemed to grow larger and larger until she whipped out her torsion blade. The steel glinted in the light. The flash made her blink. When she opened her eyes the unmoving hand returned to normal size. The pale fingers were sticking out of a plaid blanket that had been thrown over Jeff's still body. Jaden imagined that the crime scene had already been disturbed enough. Where was the knife?

She took the deepest breath possible to steady herself as she reached the last step. The pungent odor of blood made her struggle not to vomit.

The blanket hid him for a few seconds before Jaden forced herself to lift the soft corner to reveal the entire body. His light blue t-shirt was soaked with blood on the right side.

Dead as dead could be.

Someone had tried to contain the blood flow by placing rolled up towels around the top of his body. The odor of blood was almost drowned out by the sharp odor of vinegar mixed with dill. This was the bottom, actually first, floor of the house. Lined up against the far wall were six old fashioned wooden barrels that must contain Ruth's prize winning pickle factory. The wall to her right had a large stainless steel counter and extra-large sink. Hanging on the wall were several large knives graduated in size and two saws that could hardly be necessary for pickles. Curious but there must be some reason Ruth would have them. The other wall had three cupboards. There was a door, too, that must lead out to the hill under the long, tall posts that supported the house. Jaden guessed that if Ruth could have made them, there would be shelves and shelves of prize winning pickles. She felt sad that Ruth's county fair prize winners would be no more.

She did not see the weapon. The knife probably dislodged itself on the fall down the stairs. *Where was it? She searched carefully.* That was important evidence.

Jeff was dead.

She felt guilty that nothing but relief washed over her. Jaden could not think of one good reason why he should be alive. Plenty of reasons to be glad he was no longer moving. *What is the matter with me?* She forced her hands to pull down the blanket. There was no sign of another wound. He was lying on his stomach. No way was she going to touch him to turn him over. She would have to call Bill. All she could think now was that Jeff was dead. The only thing odd was the missing knife.

The suspicion that one of the knives on the wall must be the weapon used was compelling. Why would they clean the knife? Jaden closed her eyes while an uncomfortable feeling she could not shake mushroomed in her mind. The knives were hanging two flights down from where Jeff had attacked Laura.

Ruth came at him with a knife sharp enough to plunge easily right into Jeff's side. All of Ruth's knives were as sharp as Jaden could make them.

It could have come from the kitchen. She would check the knives when she went back upstairs. First, she would call MacKenzie, then Bill. Jaden took a deep breath. On her first step up suddenly her foot felt like it was nailed to the wood. She leaned against the wall to take several deep breaths. That normally always helped steady her. Maybe it was the distinctive sweet odor of blood or the heady presence of death. The whole story that Ruth and Laura told seemed true enough. God knows Jeff would never have left Laura alone.

Jeff dead was the best condition for him and for the rest of the world.

A little remorse would be more normal. Even seeing the dead body she could not feel sympathy for him. Maybe the dizziness meant she was feeling the death more deeply than she imagined. Her recovery from being trapped in the caves under the Bartlett house in Big Sur had been slow. Some days she wondered if she could get out of bed. Bill came almost every day to talk her into wellness. *Bill. She needed to call Bill. She must call MacKenzie first.* The deep breaths finally helped her move her granite like feet up the stairs. At the top she stopped again to think. *Should she question Laura herself?*

Maybe she could do it subtly.

Laura came out of the kitchen. "I made some coffee. It's a good brand from Hawaii."

Jaden felt surprised that the woman did not ask anything about her husband or the gruesome trip downstairs.

Either she did not care or she was blocking the whole incident out. *Detached.* That was it. Given the history with Jeff that was possible. Since Jaden guiltily felt relieved herself that the man was dead how could Laura's behavior be suspicious? The woman had been abused for so long that if she finally snapped that would be perfectly understandable. Maybe not too many people, but to Jaden…her mind whirled back to when she found out that Sergio had lied to her for months. The anger at betrayal consumed her.. Gradually Jaden realized she was just as angry with herself for being lonely and gullible.

Her friend, Bobbi, would understand Laura's situation. Except when Bobbi's husband attacked her, he accidentally fell on the knife. Fate. But a politically ambitious district attorney decided to try her for murder. They met when Bobbi moved into the apartment next to hers. It was months before Jaden realized that the librarian had moved to Carmel to disappear and change her life. When she marries David Bartlett she will have the ultimate getaway home.

Laura was trying to do the same thing-escape her husband and disappear. These circumstances or coincidences seemed all too familiar.

Jaden's marriage had been so happy it was hard for her to relate. She had always thought of herself as lucky. Her luck ran out when she met Sergio Manetti. After leaving her home in Nebraska to move to Carmel to be with the man, the news that he was married devastated her.

"Jaden, coffee?" Laura's voice brought Jaden out of her painful memories.

"Thank you, Laura. I'd love some." She took another deep breath. *Back to reality. Focus. Focus.*

The waft of coffee from Laura's pour made her take another deep breath. Jaden almost dived for the chair in anticipation of her first sip. "Laura, please join me," Laura hesitated for a moment and then nodded. She set the pot back on the stove and opened the walnut cupboard door to the left of the sink to take out another mug.

She poured her coffee and joined Jaden at the round oak table.

"How are you doing, Laura?" Jaden wondered if she would hear a true answer.

"Actually, I would be very happy if Ruth were not so sick."

Honest enough. "I understand," Jaden reached out to touch Laura's pale hand.

Tears welled up in Laura's clear blue, red rimmed eyes. Her hands trembled.

Jaden swallowed hard. Maybe the woman had finally come to realize what had happened to Jeff.

No, the tears were for Ruth. Laura was probably relieved that her husband was out of her life. She would not be afraid any more. How long had they been married? How long had she tolerated the beatings? Too long, Jaden thought. So long that his death was a release for the abused woman.

"It's going to be all right, Laura." That was all she could think of to say. How she wished Bobbi was with her. Bobbi would know what to say.

Jeff's legacy. Everyone who knew you is happy you are gone.

"I'll take care of her." Laura spoke softly. "She helped me so much. I will take care of her. All of her relations are gone. She does have some friends here. The people from her church are so kind. Her minister stopped by one day. A very dedicated man from the Community Christian church in Monterey."

"Pastor Wilson?"

"Yes, that's him. He invited me to church. Ruth and I were going to go when she felt better. She wasn't getting better. When I insisted she go to the doctor, Ruth told me that she had seen several doctors, all specialists."

Fresh tears filled her eyes. Her nose was red from crying about Ruth, Jaden was sure. No tears for Jeff.

It would be good if Jeff's death was determined to be an accident. Hopefully the fall down the stairs killed him. That would certainly be classified as an accident. Then maybe this all would go away. Laura could start a new life some way. And the store. She would need help getting out of the lease. What to do with the inventory? MacKenzie would be a tremendous help.

"Laura, how do you think Jeff found out you were here?"

Laura looked down at the table instead of at her. "I don't know."

Because Laura was not looking up, Jaden felt a twinge of suspicion. But the woman had been through hell and now this. "Did anyone else know you were here?"

"I can't think of anyone." She lifted her coffee mug and finally looked at Jaden through the steam as she sipped. After she set the mug down, she said, "Pastor Wilson saw me here."

"Can't believe the pastor would say anything." Jaden made a mental note that Laura was not telling her the truth or was leaving something out. Omission is a sideways type of lying. Media does it all the time. Jaden had been a communications instructor at the University of Nebraska. With all of her training and what she felt was her excellent intuition, Sergio Manetti fooled her completely. He was a womanizer and a practiced liar. Or she was just so lonely that her instincts were dulled. Jaden would never forget how she felt when Sergio came to her grand store opening for A Slice of Carmel with his wife.

Sergio's wife finally killed him.

She had to admit to herself that she understood the rage that must have led up to her husband's murder. The other murder was of an innocent man. For that there was no excuse.

Actually, if Jaden had not been the first one blamed for the murder she would have had total sympathy with the woman.

She called MacKenzie. Jaden heard her own voice trembling when the lawyer answered. "I need to tell you...."

"Is it Laura?" he interrupted.

Jaden hesitated for a moment. Finally she managed to say. "Laura is all right."

"She has been on my mind." He understandably sounded very relieved.

"Not good," she began. "Jeff, her husband, is dead. I'm here at Ruth's house. He broke in the house and was attacking Laura when Ruth stabbed him with a kitchen knife. He fell down the stairs and died. They called me first. I decided to call you before the police. I don't want to call them before we get your best legal advice."

"I'll be right over!"

"Thanks, MacKenzie." His condo was not more than a mile away. When she hung up she felt so grateful. The legal problems involved here were out of her league and she knew it. Ruth does not have long to live. Just when Laura found a place, it would be taken away from her. Jaden took a deep breath and sank to the nearest kitchen chair. She rubbed the sides of her temples hoping to stop the dull ache.

"Are you all right?" Laura asked. That jarred Jaden out of her nightmarish memories of her foolish mistake.

The honest answer would have been "no." Instead she spoke in a dull whisper, "I'm all right. Just a little headache. It will go away."

"Would you like some aspirin?"

"Thanks, Laura. If this does not go away in a while I'll try some."

Laura put an arm around her shoulders. "It's going to be all right, Jaden. Don't worry. I'm sorry you had to see *him.* Could I tell you something? It's...it's...not good."

Jaden nodded.

"I'm glad."

Jaden closed her eyes and nodded. With everything that he had done to Laura she understood perfectly. Jeff was never going to leave her alone.

When MacKenzie returned from the murder scene, he gently shook her shoulder. "You were asleep. When I said rest you took me seriously, Jaden. You need to go home."

"I feel a little better. I took some aspirin." She thought he honestly wanted to say, "You look terrible, but he was too polite.

She felt grateful that he came to help. The legal problems involved here were out of her league and she knew it. Ruth does not have long to live. Just when Laura found a place, it would be taken away from her. Jaden took a deep breath and sank to the nearest kitchen chair. She rubbed the sides of her temples hoping that would stop the nagging headache. If it did not go away quickly her only remedy would be sleep. But she needed to stay with Laura and Ruth while MacKenzie was here.

"Jaden, are you all right?" She had not even noticed Laura coming into the kitchen.

The honest answer would have been "no." Instead she said, "I'm all right. Just a little headache. It will go away soon."

MacKenzie asked, "Laura, could you show me how Jeff got into the house? "Jaden would you call the police?"

She nodded, taking her phone from her purse. Luckily the number was in her cell phone contacts. Everything looked blurry.

She heard Laura saying, "He came in the side door by breaking the glass window on top and reaching in to unlock the door."

They walked the short distance to the side door out of Jaden's sight while she explained the situation to Alma, who was taking phone calls at the Carmel station..

When they returned, MacKenzie commented, "Laura, there's no broken glass in the hallway?"

"Because I was afraid Ruth might step in some of the glass I swept it up and then vacuumed. It's in the trash."

Jaden knew the glass should have been left where it was, but she understood Laura's reasoning. The pieces of jagged amber glass were dangerous. What were the police going to think about the women cleaning the knife and sweeping up? If Jaden thought this was strange the actions certainly would not look good to investigators.

"I can't think of anyone who would know I was here except the pastor." Laura lifted her coffee mug and finally looked at Jaden through the steam as she sipped. After she set the mug down, she said, "The Pastor is the only one who saw me here except for you. He might have mentioned it to someone in passing. Maybe accidentally."

Not a good possibility. Jeff was certainly not one to hang around a church.

She shut her eyes tightly and forced herself back to the tragic reality of the moment and the future legal problems for the two innocent women.

"I'll have to call Bill now." Jaden again dug her phone out of her purse. With Bill there would be police cars and maybe reporters and who knows what else.

The phone rang several times until Jaden decided she would have to leave a message. Suddenly she heard his voice.

She breathed a sigh of relief. "Bill something terrible has happened."

"Laura?" He had the same thought as the rest of us..

Jaden told him. "Laura is all right."

"What's wrong?"

"Not good," she began. "Jeff, her husband, is dead. I'm here at Ruth's house. They called me first. He broke in the house and was attacking Laura when Ruth stabbed him with a kitchen knife. He fell down the stairs and died."

Bill's answer was a groan, then a growl, "Be there as soon as possible."

When she hung up she again felt thankful for MacKenzie. Ruth does not have long to live. What a tragedy to happen at this time. Jaden took a deep breath and sank to the nearest kitchen chair. She rubbed the sides of her temples to ease the ache.

"Jaden, are you all right?"

The honest answer would have been "No." Instead she said, "Laura, I'm sure this ache will go away soon."

"Didn't the aspirin help?"

"Thanks, Laura. If this does not go away in a few minutes I'll try some more."

Laura sat down next to her and put an arm around her shoulders. "It's going to be all right, Jaden. Don't worry. I'm sorry you had to see *him*. Could I tell you something? I'm glad."

Jaden closed her eyes and nodded. She understood. With everything that he had done to Laura she understood perfectly. Jeff was never going to leave her alone. Bill explained to her that type of personality becomes fixated on the person they feel they own. And for years Laura had let herself be dominated and beaten. Bobbi tried to explain why she stayed in her situation for several years until one day the truth hit her like a bolt of lightning. She went to an attorney right away for a divorce and a court order to keep her abusive husband away from her. In spite of that he broke into the house. That ended in tragedy that almost ruined Bobbi's life. Her husband fell attacking her with a kitchen knife. He bled to death.

Jaden's headache was getting worse. Her eyes were blurring. "Laura, I will try the aspirin. And maybe some more coffee." Laura was handing her aspirin and water when the doorbell rang. She sank back in the chair. After taking a few deep breaths she felt a little more steady. When MacKenzie walked back into the room Jaden felt relieved enough to smile.

He moved over to her right away. "Jaden, let me rub your hands. Sometimes that helps. He sat down next to her and took her hands. "Your hands are cold."

Laura offered, "I gave her some aspirin. She was getting a headache."

"Stay right here until you feel better, Jaden. Laura, please sit down, too, and tell me what happened. Tell me every detail you remember." The rubbing warmed Jaden's hands so she did feel a little better.

MacKenzie made continual notes on everything that Laura said. The whole time Jaden was fighting and losing to the headache gremlin she kept also fighting that elusive, uncomfortable feeling of something not being right. When she came into the house Jaden felt something frightening.

What could be more wrong than a dead body? *That must be it.* The shock of seeing Jeff's body downstairs, her lack of a good night's sleep, everything was pushing her into the edge of darkness from which she could not escape. For a few seconds she felt herself trapped into the clammy, wet cave underneath the Bartlett house.

The horrifying image startled her back to reality. She was in the kitchen of Ruth's home, listening to Laura tell the story again while Mackenzie was taking his meticulous notes. Her headache had vanished. She felt like going to bed and sleeping for a week.

It wasn't in the cards for today. Bill would be here soon. He would want to know why they took so long to call the police. 911 should have been called immediately. Truth was Ruth and Laura probably did not care to save Jeff.

She could not blame them. Who knows what anyone would do for self-defense in such frightening circumstances? Bobbi admitted that she deliberately stalled calling 911 after her husband fell on the knife.

Jaden remembered how furious she was when she found out that her romantic lover, Sergio, was married and a well-known womanizer...

MacKenzie snapped her back to reality, "Jaden, we're going downstairs to see the body. Then I'll speak to Ruth if she is able. The police are going to wonder about the time delay. I'm going to explain it as shock and fright. That's easy enough to explain after the abusive history of his behavior. These possessive stalkers are so dangerous. Ruth and Laura were lucky."

"They were." Jaden closed her eyes.

She felt his hand on her shoulder.

"Try to rest for a while.. Once we call the police you won't have time to rest. I won't be downstairs for long."

Jaden opened her eyes long enough to see him start down the stairs with Laura. She closed them again and put her elbows on the table to hold her head. It would just be a few moments rest.

Her head slipped off her elbows and Jaden caught herself before she hit the table. Fell asleep again. Since her almost tragedy in the caves at the Bartlett estate, her energy level was low. The knowledge of Jeff's death and viewing his body exhausted her more than she wanted to imagine. First thinking Laura was dead. Then seeing Jeff's souless body in Ruth's basement room. The saddest realization was she felt relief instead of sorrow. *What a way to be remembered.*

The police and ambulance arrived, sirens blazing. Jaden noticed a small group of people gathered on the front lawn.

MacKenzie met them. They turned and walked off the property. Of course Bill was the first person to come into the kitchen. MacKenzie was right behind him.

"Jaden, this happened yesterday evening. Why didn't anyone report it?" Bill asked as the emergency crew was heading downstairs.

"Ruth and Laura were terrified. Ruth didn't call me until this morning," Jaden protested. "I wasn't sure what to do after I heard their story. I decided to call MacKenzie. Bill, Ruth is very sick— stage four cancer."

Bill's face suddenly looked tired. "Oh, no. I'm sorry, Jaden. Knowing Jeff's history, I'm going to make an exception and interview Laura here with MacKenzie present. I'll tape the interview. When Ruth is well enough I'll do the same thing. At this point I doubt there will be any charges filed against either one of them. But I must have the story of exactly what happened." He sat down next to her and brushed her hair back over her ear. He spoke quietly, "Can you tell me what you know?"

Jaden went through the story just as Ruth told her. She could not help adding, "Why did this happen? Was there anything we could have done to prevent it?"

He hugged her. "I doubt it. The record for many of these abusers is for some reason they become obsessed. Laura's lucky. We could be investigating her death right now."

MacKenzie came into the kitchen. "I've spoken to Laura. She's sitting with Ruth right now. Bill, I would like to stay for any interviews with them. They are my clients now."

His statement made Jaden breathe a sigh of relief. The two women could not be in better hands.

Bill answered, "Of course, MacKenzie. One thing I would like right now is for Jaden to go home. She really needs rest."

Home sounded like heaven. She asked, "What if Laura needs me?"

"Laura has great help with MacKenzie. For her own good she is going to have to learn to deal with life herself. You must rest. Please take care of yourself. Do you need a ride home? I can bring your car over later."

She nodded, knowing that Bill was right. "I can drive.. It's only a few blocks. I'll leave if you promise me one thing."

Bill closed his dark eyes, "I didn't think that this was a negotiation."

She took his arm. "You won't arrest Ruth or Laura. Please."

"I don't see any reason for that. They are hardly the nation's most wanted."

MacKenzie said, "Jaden, don't worry. This is a pretty clear case of self-defense. And with Ruth's condition we can plead special medical circumstances. Bill's right. You need to rest."

"Yes. I'm glad Hal is at the shop. I'll ask him again to close for me. Thank you both for everything you are doing."

She decided to leave by the side door, using a piece of tissue to turn the knob. She must get home to sleep. Jeff did not park their car in front of Ruth's house. He wanted to sneak up on them. That area possibly might have Jeff's fingerprints.

Once outside, Jaden forced herself to walk tall and steady through the side door and walked down the black slate path across the lawn to her car. Her head was pounding. She thought she spotted Jeff's car parked several houses away. Must tell Bill. The mystery was how did Jeff find them?

Breathless, Jaden slid into the driver's seat. She saw Bill and MacKenzie standing at the front door. Her hand slid into the pocket to find her keys next to her old friend, her Monarch knife. The touch of it always calmed her. Jaden slipped the key into the ignition, waved, and drove away from Ruth's house slowly. She dredged up every bit of her remaining strength to turn onto Highway One and drive the car to the next exit, Carpenter Street. As she turned down Sixth Jaden wondered if it was possible for her to maneuver the Toyota into the entrance to their underground parking garage. She did it. Once she parked and locked the car Jaden knew that she had to see Hal before going up to her apartment.

Hal was just finishing a sale when she walked in. "Thanks so much, Mrs. Everton. Come again whenever you need those knives sharpened."

"I certainly will." The woman walked outside, obviously happy about spending her money. Hal had the knack of a great salesman. People left knowing that they had purchased the best product in the world.

"Thanks so much," he said as a beaming Mrs. Everton walked out the door .

Hal asked, "Jaden, what's wrong? You look pale."

"I'm not feeling well, Hal. You can close the shop for me today?"

"Of course." Hal came out from behind the display case and put his arm around her shoulder. "The best thing for you to do is to get to bed. Try not to worry."

"You're an angel." She left the shop and struggled up the concrete steps. Jaden had to stop twice to catch her breath. The twenty-five steps up to the apartment seemed like a hundred. Hers was the first apartment to the right with a good view of the park. She dove straight for the sofa, not even bothering to change her clothes. Everything would wait until tomorrow. MacKenzie would call her. Bill would come over. She wanted to tell Bobbi what had happened. It was too similar to what Bobbi had gone through. Jaden hesitated, not wanting to upset her friend. Right now she was too exhausted to even talk. She had spoken to Laura at Ruth's. *You won't have to be afraid. You have friends now. Me. Ruth. MacKenzie, Bobbi....*

. She did need to pull off her shoes to keep the sofa clean. When Jaden yanked off her shoes her forefinger felt like it had been stung. Blood dripped from the inside of her finger to her thumb. What? Jaden turned her shoe over to look at the sole. Two small, jagged pieces of glass were stuck in her heel. She lay on her back on the couch and pressed on the small cut until it stopped bleeding. Everything went black for a few seconds. She opened her eyes to see the bleeding was stopped. Jaden looked down at the soles of her shoes. When did she step on glass? What should she do with the shards? Ask to have them tested? Why? There was no overwhelming evidence that this amber glass had anything to do with anything. This afternoon she could have stepped on broken glass on any sidewalk.

Laura cleaned the hallway thoroughly so Ruth would not accidentally step on the shattered glass.

She must have picked up the broken glass walking to her car. That nagging feeling of something not being quite right pushed itself to the front of her mind. What was it? Jaden squeezed her eyes shut and immediately fell asleep.

Jaden woke in the dark. She breathed deeply, grateful that her head no longer pounded. The monstrous headache was gone. Her eyes were no longer blurry so she could see that the digital kitchen clock read two a. m. Seven hours of sleep did the trick.

Her finger still stung. How did she get that glass in her shoe?

"Have to get that glass out of the soles." Barefoot, she stood up to get a pair of tweezers from the bathroom.

Jaden took a plate from the kitchen cupboard to hold the shoe while she carefully pulled the three pieces of amber glass from her sole. She stared down at the soles of her shoes. When did she step on glass? It had to be outside. The only way it would be outside was if the window in the top part of the door was hit from *inside* the house. That told Jaden more than she wanted to know. Clear glass could be anywhere. Amber glass was not that common. Her grandparents had an amber glass window. Their house was built in the 1960s.

.The events of the day were jumping trampoline style all around her. For a moment Jaden wished her friend, Bobbi, was here. This tragedy would not be the best story for her. This was eerily similar to what had happened to the woman. In spite of a court order her husband broke into the house. He tried to kill her with a knife he had brought with him. In the struggle he fell on the blade. An eager DA who wanted to run for senator tried her for murder.

"This never should have come to trial," MacKenzie repeated to any media that would interview him. The stories of abuse gained tremendous public sympathy.

After the trial Bobbi only wanted to disappear. She altered her name and came to Carmel for a new life. What Jaden found out later was that Bobbi was deliberately placed in Apartment Number 2 so Bill in Number 3 could keep an eye on her. This was arranged through the mayor, who knew the librarian's real identity. He had reservations about her innocence. "Just to be on the safe side...." he told Bill. Only Bill and his captain knew Bobbi's real identity.

Yawning, she left the plate with four glass shards and the shoe on the counter.

Bed never felt as good as it did when she flopped on the bedroom quilt. She did not have enough strength to slip under the covers. *Sleep, sleep please come.* But she could not keep what had happened at Ruth's buried long enough to go back to sleep.

Ruth's shaky voice suddenly filled the room. "No, Jaden, I've made sure that he would never bother her again. I promised he would not hurt her ever. I made sure of it when I killed him. I've written my signed confession. I did not hesitate before. There's just one thing that I want you to do."

Jaden heard herself answering, "What is it, Ruth?"

"I need to have you make sure that the downstairs will be closed. Laura is not going to be making pickles. Just make sure that no one goes down there. The brine can last a long time. Or it could be tossed into the ocean, no, maybe the dump."

Why was she talking about pickles when Jeff was killed in her house? Her illness must be the explanation. It was like worrying about a puddle during a rainstorm.

I can't help what the police might do. But I can't imagine why they would bother with the pickle barrels. Jaden's stomach knotted. Something was wrong here. It was Ruth saying "before." She might not have meant to say it. The terminally ill woman was taking a lot of pain medication. This had been a nightmare experience for her. She tried to help someone and it turned out wrong. If only Jeff had not found out where his wife was.

His finding where Laura was might forever be a mystery.

Maybe there was some clue in their car, which she noticed was still parked two houses away from Ruth's. After she had said goodbye to Ruth and Laura she decided to go out the side door, down the black slate walkway through the grass to the car. It was unlocked. She made a mental note to herself to tell Laura that the car should be locked.

All of this spun in her head when she was trying to go to sleep. She was thinking of warming some milk when her body finally relaxed enough to enter the unknown, the dark tunnel of sleep.

Jaden had not heard from her lawyer or Bill about the final decision of the district attorney for over a week. The store kept her busy enough. For that she was grateful. Keeping up with her work proved a godsend. About two weeks later MacKenzie finally called.

He explained, "I already have an appointment with the District Attorney. With everything that happened to Laura the killing can be secondary to the trauma she experienced for years. Ruth's illness is terminal cancer. Her statement is a deathbed confession. The public would hate anyone who persecuted them. Jeff was a wife beater who would not stop stalking Laura .He broke into the house to attack her. Ruth saw what was happening and ran for a knife. Stabbed Jeff's side to make him stop.

He died from the fall down the stairs. He did not bleed to death.

Jaden hoped it would be considered accidental although she knew the stabbing certainly caused the deadly fall."

"That's what I suspected. That has to be a self-defense plea," Jaden whispered. She prayed that was the correct conclusion.

MacKenzie told her, "Harder to explain is the cleanup. They cleaned the knife and the glass from the broken door pane. Trauma can explain it. They were overwhelmed and didn't know they were destroying evidence. Jeff died from the fall. Ruth could not even say what knife she used. After tests the police lab finally found it. The sharpest knife they had ever seen.

She thanked, MacKenzie over and over. Laura had been through so much. She deserves some peace in her life. And Ruth needs to have peace for the rest of the short time she has left. Though her life has been difficult, she's never complained. And Ruth gave Laura a home. Someone she barely knew offered her hope.

"Really? No relation?" MacKenzie had questioned her.

"No. Pure generosity. Some people have a special compassion gene. Ruth does."

"Then it's too bad that there aren't more people in the world like her."

"There are people who follow the open door policy.' If anyone comes to my door I will invite them in.'"

MacKenzie smiled and answered, "Because they might be visiting angels."

Jaden sighed. "Laura came to Ruth's door. She was someone who needed help. You helped me when I was suspected of murder. You certainly helped Bobbi. As for your fee...."

"I think in this case I will donate my legal services. It's a good cause."

"MacKenzie, thank you. There is no way either Laura or Ruth could afford your services. The gift shop is bankrupt."

"You're welcome, Jaden. Now, I want you to do something for me."

"Anything, MacKenzie."

"You're not getting enough rest. It has not been that long ago that you were in a sick bed. Although I'm not a physician my prescription would be a vacation."

"That sounds perfect. I wish I had gone yesterday. I feel like this is a nightmare."

"When this is over, then." He smiled. "I know someone who would like to take you on a vacation, besides me, that is."

If she had her choice, Jaden realized going away with Bill was something she wanted to do. The truth came slowly. Some voice inside said softly, *Don't wait much longer to tell him.*

She needed to speak to Bill when they could find a private moment.

"I really appreciate what you have done, MacKenzie. How can I ever repay you?" Her damming story about the broken glass chards and Ruth's repeated confession refused to come out.

"I'll keep you informed after I see the District Attorney. If he doesn't take these circumstances into account he's going to be as popular as yellow jackets at a picnic. Since he has big ambitions he will not want any negative publicity."

"Do you think so?"

"Since Bobbi's trial I can get a crowd at a news conference. The DA knows that."

When she hung up Jaden sighed deeply. MacKenzie made her feel as though everything would work out.

Jaden knew that her jumbled feelings about Jeff's death might haunt her forever. What should she do?

"I'll fix myself some tea and toast to settle my stomach." She had just put two pieces of bread in the toaster when there was a knock at the door.

Bobbi came in and immediately hugged her. She said, "You look beat."

"I am."

"Sit down." She turned and picked up a thermos from outside the door. "I made you some chicken noodle soup. My super supper specialty."

"I didn't know that. A tongue twister."

"Actually I opened a can, but put a lot of extra chicken in it. Chicken noodle is always in my cupboard. They are never liberal with the chicken. It's like they used one chicken for 200 cans."

"Smells good." Jaden almost laughed.

Bobbi took two bowls from the cupboard and ladled out the soup. "We'll have this and your toast. And do you have any crackers?"

"Thank you, Bobbi. No crackers. I haven't been to the store."

"Do you feel like telling me what's happened up to date?"

"How much time do you have? This is going to upset you especially. I was trying to think of a way to avoid explaining."

Bobbi took two spoons from the drawer next to the sink and sat down. "Go ahead. Tell me whatever's happened."

Jaden's first bite of the warm, satisfying soup helped her relax. "That's almost as good as Sydney's clam chowder."

Bobbi answered with a laugh. "It may be the next Mad Hatter's menu item."

They both laughed.

"Thank you, Bobbi, for being such a good friend. I hope what I have to tell you doesn't upset you too much."

Jaden went through the whole story slowly and carefully to make sure she was relating accurately. She left out the glass and Ruth's admission. It was eerily similar to Bobbi's story she wondered how many women had lived through these nightmares.

. Tears welled up in her friend's lovely golden flecked eyes.

"That poor woman," Jaden whispered. "I know. If only she had left him the first time he hit her. I've tried to figure out why she didn't leave."

Bobbi's voice choked up, "It's not that easy to leave. I thought my memories were buried."

"I wondered if I should tell you at all. Too many women have gone through stories like this."

Bobbi dipped herself another ladle of soup. "If Mackenzie says he thinks the case will be dismissed soon it probably will. Leave the speculations to history. I know how difficult it is for you to let go. Think about what would be best for the future for Laura and for Ruth's memory."

"I understand. Bobbi, thank you."

"There's something else I wanted to ask you," Bobbi spoke quietly. "I've made a decision. I'm going to marry David in May Would you be my maid of honor?"

"Oh, that's wonderful. Of course."

"I've been trying to decide. Finally I admitted that he is so much a part of my life. I can't imagine being without him. It will be a big change living at the Bartlett estate. Getting away from the world is not at all bad. Has some good points."

Jaden hugged her.

"Bobbi, I know you and David are going to be so happy.

"Thank you, Jaden. Now tell me how things are between you and Bill."

Jaden sighed, "About the same."

"When you two are together Bill rarely takes his eyes off of Jaden Steele. Do you realize that he loves you? When you were in the hospital recovering he was so different--nervous and distracted. Not his usual self."

She had not thought about a future with Bill like Bobbi was planning her future with David.

"You're frowning. Do you love him?"

Her friend would have made an excellent lawyer. She finally nodded her head. He was so different from her first husband, Brent, who had been her best friend from high school on. Bill brought out passionate feelings in her that were actually frightening. After the initial fright she would relax and smile to herself.

"I'm not going to say any more. You can think for yourself." Bobbi said with a smile, "Good night and pleasant dreams."

As long as she was thinking of Bill she would have pleasant dreams. *Bobbi is right. Admit it. What reason is there to keep quiet? Look at how happy Bobby is. Her first marriage was a disaster. Now she is really...really...on top of the world.*

Jaden was always happier with Bill around. When he walked into the apartment the whole atmosphere changed. When he left she always wanted to ask him to come back. *And I love him but it's different. With Brent she was comfortable.*

Jaden fell asleep with Bill's image in front of her closed eyes.

In the morning she called Ruth's house.

Laura answered. "I'm so sorry it's been two weeks since I called and three since I've been over. Can I come to say hello to Ruth?"

"Oh, she would love that. She is getting weaker and weaker. Jaden," she heard the tremor in Laura's voice. "The doctor says sometime this month we should be thinking of calling hospice."

"I'm should see her, Laura. What would be a good time for me to come? Could I bring some chowder for you from The Mad Hatter's Café?"

"Thank you, Jaden. Soup is about all she can handle. Sometimes she can't even finish that."

"I'll close the shop early and be over about four thirty."

"All right. We will see you then."

The smell of the warm chowder filled her car as she drove over to Ruth's cul-de-sac at the end of Sea Breeze Court.

Jaden was tempted to take the path to the side door to see if she could spot any glass chards. The soup was a handicap along with a container of crackers and cookies that Sydney threw in plus her purse, which normally weighed five pounds. The extra food added at least a pound. She walked up the front path and had to put down the soup to ring the doorbell.

Laura answered immediately. "I'm so glad you came. She was so excited when I told her. She's been writing you a thankyou note." She took the container of chowder and walked down the hall with Jaden to the kitchen.

"Laura, I'm so sorry. I've known Ruth ever since I moved to Carmel. She will always be the sweet lady who brought the beautiful, colorful orchids to the shop."

"She's been a savior to me. I don't know what I would have done without her taking me into her home." Tears spilled down her cheeks.

Jaden hugged her.

"I've been crying at night when Ruth couldn't see me."

"Do you have help?"

"There's a nurse coming every afternoon. She's wonderful."

Jaden removed the container from its brown paper bag. "Hot."

Laura took down three bowls from the cabinet next to the kitchen sink. "Go see Ruth while I get things ready. I'll bring a bowl in for her."

"Thanks, Laura." Jaden thought, *back to reality,* as she walked to Ruth's room. She passed the repaired window in the side door. The glass was clear, probably so you could see who was standing outside No more amber glass.

"Hello, Jaden," a thin voice rose from the bed. She was sitting up with two pillows propped behind her. To Jaden she looked paler and smaller than ever. She reached out for her hand, which was icy cold. Jaden automatically rubbed them.

"I get very cold now," Ruth admitted. "You see I have two blankets. I'm still cold. It must be poor circulation from lying in this bed. It's very hard to get up now. Laura or the nurse has to help me do anything."

"Ruth, I'm so sorry."

"Don't be. I've had a busy life if not the perfect one you might wish for. And I was able to help Laura."

"Taking her in was a wonderful thing."

"How could I not?"

Why should Jaden be so suspicious of this dear old woman?

"I want to repeat my story about Jeff's death to you, Jaden. I've written it all down.

150

Laura brought me some paper. I stabbed the man because he was attacking Laura. She had nothing to do with it."

This was as close to a death bed statement as possible. But Jaden had to ask.

"How do you think that Jeff found out that Laura was here?"

Ruth closed her eyes. When she opened them an eerie smile crossed her face.

"Can you guess? I think you can."

Jaden hesitated and finally decided to say, "You or Laura called him."

"I thought we set it up very well. That was the only thing we could not figure out at first. Finally Laura borrowed the phone at the Elks Club. It's only two blocks from here. He deserved to die for what he had done to Laura for years. He never would have stopped. I did it before, you know. The second time is much easier. You see my husband was a brute, too. Killing him turned out to be a pleasure. I just could not make another body disappear. I wasn't physically strong enough."

Jaden could not move or speak for several seconds. Thoughts in her mind started to spin like an out of control carousel. Ruth planned Jeff's murder. Jeff would have disappeared like Ruth's husband years earlier. Everyone would have been so happy that they might not have even bothered to search for the man. Jaden actually felt the vibration of screams from the ghosts downstairs.

She thought the gloom she felt down there was seeing Jeff's body. Now she realized why she needed to escape from the downstairs of this house. And Ruth, the dear, sweet old woman was a killer.

Ruth seemed to be reading her thoughts. "I am responsible. You must make everyone understand that. Here's my note." With pale, shaking hands she took a paper from under her pillow and handed it to Jaden. "Keep this. Laura is not to blame. She was distraught and terrified, easy to manipulate into helping me."

Jaden stared at the note. Finally she stuffed it in her purse.

"You understand, don't you?"

"Yes, I think I do." She took Ruth's cold hand again. "Can I...can I do anything else for you?"

"Yes. Laura won't be making any pickles. Those pickle barrels could be dumped taken to the dump as is. Do you understand me, Jaden? I would like to have my ashes scattered at sea."

Jaden understood more than she wished she did. Ruth was giving her the responsibility of getting rid of some damming evidence. The secret spice. Her stomach seemed to flip over."

"Will do," she whispered, wishing she were anywhere but here. I'll be back soon."

"Thank you, Jaden."

Jaden could barely look at Laura when she went back to the kitchen.

"I feel so badly for her," Laura said.

"I do, too. But she will be in a better place. I see her in a garden happily tending the orchids."

"Do you think so?"

"Yes, I do," she lied.

"You are sp thoughtful.."

152

Jaden did her best to stand upright and walk to the car as fast as she could. She had to get away from that house. Now she knew that besides Jeff's death there had been another murder in that house.

In spite of her first memories of the house with its rainbow myriad of orchids I hope I never have to step into that place again.

They asked Jeff to the house. They plotted the entire murder. If Laura was not the original planner she went along with the deadly trick. Jaden felt her reasoning was correct but there was no proof. A few pieces of glass that could have come from anywhere. Now the remaining pieces of the amber glass window were no more.

The drive back to the apartment confused her more than ever. A certainty would be to always remember the moment when she realized that almost everything she thought about Ruth for two years was an illusion.

Back in her own apartment she decided to make herself a cup of calming tea--chamomile was best for her. She loved breathing in the warm aroma. She closed her eyes and took a few deep, calming breaths.

A picture of Laura lying in the hospital bed came to her. Something she would never forget. The doctor outlined her older injuries, too. Bobbi tried to explain why abused people keep quiet. They are made to feel that the problem is their fault.

As far as Jaden was concerned someone like Jeff could have been dropped in the ocean to see if he could swim back.

Her problem was knowing the truth. What should she do?

The phone's sharp ring broke into her speculation. The sound of Bill's voice made her immediately happy. How lucky she was to have him in her life.

"Hi, beautiful lady. How are you?"

"Tired. I just saw Ruth. Her time is short. Laura is going to call hospice soon."

"I'm so sorry, Jaden. She was a sweet old gal. I don't know if MacKenzie has called you yet. The District Attorney is not filing any case. He understands that Ruth will be gone soon and that Laura had been abused for years."

"That is good news," Jaden answered.

"I'd like to come over when my shift is finished. Would that be alright?"

"Of course."

Nothing would make her happier.

Except should she be honest with him? Ruth's words ran over and over in her mind like an old fashioned record that stuck in one grove. Ruth was two personalities. One was a dear, sweet old woman who took in an abused victim who came to her door. She brought her lovely orchids to the shops in Carmel all these years. The other Ruth planned the way to get rid of someone no one else would miss. Laura did not plan the killing but she participated. She called Jeff, invited him to the house knowing exactly what the two women would do. Neither of them would be charged.

Could Jaden justify the murder? Two murders if she was going to be honest with herself. She stared at the small white dish in the counter. The sun was hitting the shards so they sparkled like gold. She imagined what a sharp lawyer like MacKenzie would destroy that speculation. A sweet old woman almost dead and the wife who endured years of abuse.

Sometime one has to make difficult choices that might frustrate blind justice.

She picked up the dish and let the golden chips slide into the trash. She smiled.

Jaden did not know why she was smiling. Maybe there was an abnormal streak in her, too. Ruth was a dear sweet orchid lady to the merchants in Carmel. Her other self was a dangerous killer. The orchid lady's note that Jaden pulled out of her purse tore beautifully into a hundred pieces. It was now a beautiful celebration confetti.

She imagined that many people had secrets that they would keep to themselves for their entire lives. The decision was made. It was the best one for all concerned. The true story would be buried as deeply as the souls in the Carmel graveyard. The murders could never be justified.

Jaden did not have to explain or excuse her actions in shoveling the truth with Jeff's coffin. She would never speak of the real story for the rest of her life.

What would she have done if Ruth were not sick and dying? Luckily she would never have that choice. Ruth would always be a dear sweet orchid lady. Only she and Laura would know the truth.

First she would call MacKenzie and thank him again. Then she would call Bill. She only had one thing to tell him.

That would change their lives. Now she knew how happy that would make her. And she wanted to make him happy. As for her secret knowledge about the events on Seabreeze Court, she closed her eyes. In the sea of green grass, Jaden saw a graveyard.

A sober gray, overgrown tombstone read,
Secrets buried here

LITTLE MISS MUPPET

A Jaden Steele Carmel Mystery

Barbara Chamberlain

Patti, the children's librarian was sick. Jaden always enjoyed filling in because she loved to read. Bobbi had called that they were really shorthanded. There were about a dozen eager children sitting on the floor of the childrens' room. One little girl with curly brown hair was sitting in the back on a chair by the door to the room because she had brought her dog with her. She did not seem to mind being isolated, probably because the dog was keeping her company. He was a beautiful border collie with a three fourths black face that covered his left eye.

When story time was over Jaden handed out graham crackers to the audience. The little girl broke hers in half and gave it to the dog. They both swallowed their halves of the cracker in a couple of huge bites.

The other parents and children left except for the girl with the curly brown hair.

Jaden went over to her. "Is your mother coming to pick up you and your dog?

"No," the little voice trembled slightly. My mother is gone to heaven."

"I'm so sorry. Can we call someone else for you, Janelle?"

"I don't want to go home." She leaned toward Jaden and whispered. "They want to kill me and Pirate. I know it."

Jaden took in a sharp breath. She thought for a moment. Whether it was true or not the girl seemed to believe what she was saying. Her deep brown eyes were steady but brimming with tears. She kept her hand on the dog's head. Her love for Pirate was obvious. What should Jaden do now? She took a Kleenex from the box on the desk and handed it to the child.

"My name is Jaden. What's yours?"

"Janelle."

"How pretty," she answered the girl with a forced smile. She would call Bill. He was on patrol in the village. Jaden had to wonder if somehow she invited strange happenings to interrupt her life. Out of nervousness she twisted the engagement ring on the fourth finger of her left hand.

Jaden walked away so Janelle could not hear and explained her unusual conversation.

"I'll be right over."

"O.K." she walked back to Janelle. "A friend is going to come over and talk to us."

"Your friend?"

"He is my friend. He is also a Carmel policeman. He helps people."

"I wanted to talk to a policeman. My daddy always said if I needed help to call 911 and ask for police help."

"Is your daddy home?"

"No. He went on a business trip to Argentina and disappeared."

"Who lives at your house?"

"My aunt and uncle, but they want to kill us."

"Why do you think that?"

"Because I heard them last night when I went to the kitchen for a glass of milk. I got so scared that I ran back to my bedroom. I couldn't sleep so early in the morning I fixed us a bowl of cereal, got dressed, and started to walk to the library."

Bill's tall frame filled the entry to the children's room.

"Hi, Jaden. Can you introduce me?"

"This is Janelle and Pirate."

'I'm very glad to meet you." He patted the dog's head.

"I'm really glad to see a policeman," Janelle answered. "My daddy said you would be safe with a policeman."

"Janelle, would you tell Policeman Bill what you told me?"

Janelle repeated the story.

Jaden sensed that Janelle believed everything she was saying. She felt the girl was telling the truth as she knew it.

Bill sat in silence. Once he opened his mouth to say something and then shook his head. Finally he asked, "Jaden, would you come over to the desk with me for just a minute?"

"We will be right back. I'm going to give you each two crackers. Janelle was trying to be polite but whisked them out of Jaden's hand.

At the desk Bill whispered, "She has a great imagination. We have to call social services. They will investigate."

"Do we have to?"

"Of course. We can't just keep her. She probably got in trouble for something at home. Afraid she would get a spanking or some other punishment from whoever is watching her."

"Bill, she believes every word."

"Children with lively imaginations sometimes believe they have a friend that no one else can see."

"How about this. Could you check for missing persons? We can at least take her to the Mad Hatters for lunch. I would really like to talk to her some more to see if her story changes."

"O.K. But if she has been reported missing we have to talk her back. But I will question the family."

"She says her mother is dead and her father is missing in South America."

"That's enough trauma to make a child disturbed. If only we knew her last name."

Jaden stared at Janelle, who kept one arm over Pirate's neck. That familiar dark cloud misted over her vision. Something was wrong. If anything happened to this beautiful little girl she would never forgive herself.

"Janelle, would you like to come to a restaurant for lunch?"

"Oh, yes," A broad smile crossed Janelle's face. "Do they have some dog food for Pirate?"

"Well," Jaden thought. "They have a bowl of dog biscuits. And I have some hamburger in my apartment. It's right over the restaurant."

"Pirate says O.K."

Kyle greeted them as they entered Dolores Street Court. Welcome. Who is your guest and the beautiful border collie?"

Jaden answered, "This is Janelle and Pirate. My guess is that they will really appreciate lunch."

For a moment a frown wrinkled Kyle's forehead. Then he quickly went back to his smiley self. "We have dog biscuits on the menu plus anything you want."

"Clam chowder," Janelle said. "We've been here before, with my daddy."

"I recognized you," Kyle told them.

Look for Little Miss Muppet in 2021

ABOUT THE AUTHOR'

The Jaden Steele Mystery Series is set in the Monterey Bay area of California. The *Edge of Carmel* is the fourth mystery in the series. The first novel is *A Slice of Carmel* and the second Jaden Steele Mystery, *Slash and Turn introduces a* Russian ballet company whose members are the target of a murderer. The *Edge of Carmel* traps Jaden in an impossible situation. She has a difficult choice to make.

Barbara won first place in the juvenile/young adult category of the Writers Digest Competition for her original fable set in Okinawa, *A Bowl of Rice,* in 2009.

Barbara's first novels, *Ride the West Wind* and *The Prisoner's Sword*. They were named Recommended Reading by the National Council of Teachers of English.

If you like ghost stories, check out the Ghost Town Project on the website of Anotherlanguage.org. Her story, *Canyon of Gold*, is set in Bullion Canyon, Utah.

Barbara has taught storytelling and creative writing classes. At a genealogy conference she facilitated a session, Telling Your Own Stories; Magic Through Memories.

As an elementary school librarian at Bradley Elementary School she set up three different libraries. Barbara also worked in youth services and reference at Monterey City Library and Harrison Memorial Library in Carmel. While working in Carmel she developed the concept for The Jaden Steele Mysteries set in the fascinating Monterey Bay area.

The University of California at Santa Cruz awarded Barbara a bachelor's degree. She received her Masters degree in Library and Information Science from San Jose University. She is a past president of the Northern California Pen Women and is a member of the Santa Clara County Branch. She served as District Governor of Lions District 4C6. She and her husband, Dave, live in Aptos, California.

www.ingramcontent.com/pod-product-compliance
Lightning Source LLC
Chambersburg PA
CBHW070034260626
47159CB00005B/2034